Adventures from the Coldest Part of the Cold War

A DEWLiner's Memoires – 1960-63

Brian (Simon) Jeffrey

Contents

Acknowledgements 6

Prologue 7
   What Was It All About 7
Chapter 1: What's a Cold War? 9
Chapter 2: What's a DEWLine? 11
   The DEWLine World 12
   Welcome to the DEWLine 12
Chapter 3: Getting Hired 15
Chapter 4: The Adventure Begins 19
   Getting Trained 19
   Middle of Nowhere 20
   Northward Bound 22
   A Barren Land 23
   Auxiliary (Aux) Sites 24
Chapter 5: Story Time... 29
   The Fishing Expedition..29
   Saturday Night in the Arctic...30
   Movie Time...32
   Christmas at the Real Pelly Bay 33
   Christmas at CAM-4 34
   Drag Racing 35
   The Case of the Missing Scotch 36
   Missed Boogie (Target)..37
   Working in the Dark...39
   Other Talents (or lack thereof) 40
   No Days Off..42
   Calling Santa Claus – Adventures of VE8SK...................43
   A Woman's Voice..44
   Escape from the North 45

Not Much Pay...46

Being Bushy...46

Returning North..47

Time to Move On...48

Working Around the Clock 51

Lesson Learned 52

Doctor Brian 53

The Dancing Washing Machine 55

King of the Northwest Mounted Police............................56

No Rest for the Wicked 59

Now That's Cold!...60

A Time Management Lesson 61

Time to Move Along Again...61

Here We Go Again 62

Movie Time (Part 2)...63

God's Will 64

The BOPSR Club 66

Another Kind of Freezing 67

Going Crazy 68

The Ghost at the Airfield 70

Idle Hands (and Minds) at Play......................................73

The Top of the Mountain 75

The Great Polar Bear Hunt 76

Foxes, Foxes, Everywhere 78

Becoming an Old Hand...78

One Last Time...79

Home Again 79

More Scientific Experiments 81

The Cuban Missile Crisis 82

Talking to SAC (B-52 Bombers).....................................83

Tactical Call Signs...85

Dealing with Death 85

A Movie to Remember 86

Chapter 6: All Good Things Must Come to an End **89**

Chapter 7: Post DEWLine **91**

Chapter 8: The End of the Story **93**

Postscript 93

Chapter 9: Return to the DEWLine - 2012 .... **95**

The Dream 95

Rekindled Dream 96

The Stars Align 97

Like a Child on Christmas Eve 97

The Journey of a Lifetime (for Me) 98

Chapter 10: Trip Diary **99**

Day 1: July 1 2012 - Canada Day, The Journey Begins 99

First Stop: Iqaluit 99

Day 2: July 2, 2012 - On to Hall Beach 100

Arriving at Hall Beach 101

First Look Around (in 52 years!) 102

Accommodations 103

The Electronic Modules 104

End of a Long day 104

Day 3: July 3, 2112 - First Full Day 105

Exploring the Module Trains 107

Exploring Outside 109

Day 4: July 4, 2012 - Time to Leave (Again) 110

Final Observations 111

Inuit Wisdom 111

Southward Bound 112

The Final Chapter: Historical Timeline **113**

About the Author **115**

Acknowledgements

I want to acknowledge DEWLiners Paul Kelley, Lyall Lalonde, and Clive Beckmann, whose fellowship truly exemplifies the bond that exists among DEWLiners.

I want to thank DEWLiners, Martin Allinson, Ron Blessin, Pat Carr, Mort Doyle, James Kizak, Chris Klassen, Ron Kovach, Rino Manarin, Pat Paterson, Marion Rocko, Fred Sue, Fred Teeter, Wayne Trylinski and Derek Whitehead for providing information and support over the years.

Also, a thank you to honorary DEWLiner Mark Pimlott who inadvertently started the process that saw me return to the Line in 2012. That trip to Hall Beach, FOX Main, is chronicled in chapter 10.

And an apology and thank you for the many other DEWLiners who have contacted me over the years and who's names are lost or forgotten. I'm truly sorry that your names are not listed here.

Finally, a huge "Thank You" to a non-DEWLiner Larry Wilson for the monumental task in putting together what has become "THE" website to visit when looking for information on the DEWLine. Proceeds from the sale of this book go towards maintaining that site.

You can visit the site at:

http://lswilson.dewlineadventures.com/

Prologue

What Was It All About

"From today's perspective (2006), some forty-five years older, my time spent on the Distant Early Warning (DEW) Line amounted to less than 5% of my life. Strange this small percentage should occupy so much of my memories, stranger still, some of my oldest friends to this day are DEWLiners. We probably owe our bond to sharing a unique experience and the conviction that nothing before or since has equaled it."

~ DEWLiner DeWitt Thompson II, in 2006 (deceased)

What was the Cold War? What is a DEW Liner? What was the DEWLine? Why should you care? Many people have forgotten why the period from 1947 to the early 1990s was called the Cold War and its impact on the world.

This is the true story of one person's involvement in a very small part of what was known as the Cold War. That small part was about a group of people who watched over the North American continent from radar sites in the far north. Without knowing why, the population of North America probably slept a little bit better during the Cold War because of this small band of people known as DEW Liners.

My name is Brian Jeffrey, although my name when I was on the DEWLine was Brian Simon, Simon being my adopted surname. I changed back to my birth name, Jeffrey, after leaving the DEWLine.

I had been known as Brian Simon from about the age of six, so anyone who worked with me on the DEWLine or who went to school with me in those early years will have no idea who Brian Jeffrey is. It's the ultimate witness protection program

I served on the DEWLine as a Radician (radar technician) from July 1960 to March 1963 when I went south, supposedly for the last time. I wrote the first draft of this book in 2008, and the contents became the basis for my personal DEWLine website at www.DEWLINE.ca. This final version continues the stroll down one person's memory lane with all the inaccuracies and embellishments that come with the passing of time.

I took the poetic license of titling the book "Adventures from…" as I thought the use of the term "Boring Tales from…" might be a turn off. The fact is that while I did have a few true adventures, what you'll read here is simply what life on isolated radar stations way above the Arctic Circle was like, warts and all.

I fully realize that while this book will be primarily of interest to other DEWLiners who have shared similar experiences, I sincerely hope that non-DEWLiners will find it interesting and have a few chuckles at some of the "adventures."

DEWLiners were truly Cold War warriors who worked and lived in the Coldest part of the Cold War. We are a dying breed of individual and I hope that this effort might inspire other DEWLiners to also share their experiences.

Chapter 1: What's a Cold War?

The term Cold War refers to the post-World War II geopolitical tensions between the world's two major powers, the Soviet Union and the United States. The term has been attributed to American financier and US presidential advisor Bernard Baruch. The Cassell Companion to Quotations cites a speech Baruch gave in April 16, 1947 in which he said, *"Let us not be deceived: we are today in the midst of a cold war."*

So, what does the term "Cold War" mean? Probably the best explanation I ever heard was from a 12-year-old who was part of my tour group at the Diefenbunker, Canada's Cold War Museum, where I'm a volunteer guide. In response to my question to the group, *"Who know why it was called the Cold War?"* responded, *"Because it was fought in the winter."* As the laugher died down, I began to realize that enough time had passed since the Cold War ended that many people have all but forgotten about it, and that very few people knew why the term "Cold War" came about.

Basically, the time span between 1947 and 1991 was called the Cold War because, unlike "hot wars," the two major antagonists, the Soviet Union and the United States, did not fire any weapons at each other, or engage in any formal battles. There were certainly many lives lost over the course of the Cold War but none in formal battles.

World Wars 1 and 2, the Korean War, the Vietnam War, and the Gulf War would be considered "hot wars" because weapons were used, battles were fought, and many lives were lost. It's interesting to note that two of those wars, the Korean and Vietnam wars, occurred during the Cold War period.

Chapter 2: What's a DEWLine?

What is a DEWLine, you ask? Good question. DEW stands for Distant Early Warning. The DEWLine was a chain of 61 manned, early warning radar stations that stretched across the northern part of the North American continent from Alaska to Greenland, roughly along the 69th parallel, about 125 to 190 miles (200 to 300 kilometres) north of the Arctic Circle. There were six Main stations, 27 Auxiliary stations, and 28 Intermediate stations. Most of these stations were in Canada.

The Main and Auxiliary stations (Aux Sites) were spaced across the Arctic at approximately 100-mile (160 Km) intervals with an Intermediate station (I-Site) stuck between each of the other sites. I'll provide additional information on the stations shortly.

Construction of the DEWLine began around 1955 and took 32 months to complete. It was a true engineering and construction feat. It became operational in August 1957 and most stations were decommissioned by 1994. In fact, most or all the intermediate sites had been decommissioned by the end of 1963. Some of the remaining original Auxiliary sites and Main stations morphed into the Northern Warning System (NWS) starting in 1985.

The DEWLine is a relic of the Cold War. Only a few stations remain as a reminder of those tense times when the USSR and the USA stood nose-to-nose in a war where no weapons were fired.

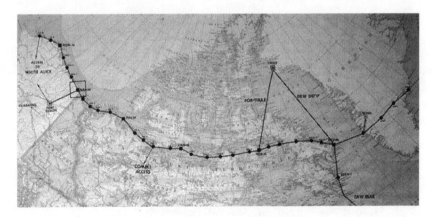

The DEWLine World

The DEWLine, also affectionally known as just the "Line," was divided into six "sectors" which were named, from West to East, POW, BAR, PIN, CAM, FOX, and DYE sectors. In turn, each sector had 2-6 Aux-Sites and 2-7 I-Sites associated with them. Aux-Sites took on the name of the Main station to its West followed by a number. For example, Aux-Sites to the East of CAM Main became CAM 1 thru 5. I spent my first year on the Line at CAM-4. I-Sites also took on the name of the Main Site to its West but added a letter identifier, A thru E. I spent several months at CAM-D.

Each DEWLine station also had a geographical name in addition to its DEWLine name. Here is a list of the geographical names associated with the six Main sites;

POW Main: Point Barrow, Alaska
BAR Main: Barter Island, Alaska
PIN Main: Cape Parry, NWT
CAM Main: Cambridge Bay, NWT
FOX Main: Hall Beach NWT
DYE Main: Cape Dyer, NWT.

The geographical name for the site where I spent most of my time, CAM-4, was Pelly Bay, NWT. The geographical name for CAM-D was Simpson Lake, NWT.

Welcome to the DEWLine

When you entered the DEWLine world in the early years, you ended up at one of three types of stations. You either stayed at one of the six Main Sites, were shipped off to one of the 27 Aux Sites or, if you were unlucky enough, you ended up at an I-Site.

The stations themselves were constructed as module trains. A basic module was a standalone unit, 28 by 16 by 10 feet tall. The modules were then connected side by side to form a module train. One way to visualize a module train is to dump a box of dominos on a table and then line them up side by side on the long side.

The largest of the DEWLine stations, the six Main Sites, consisted of two parallel, 25 module long trains (400 feet long by 28 feet wide) connected by an overhead enclosed bridge. The Main Sites would have been staffed by 45 civilians of which 7-8 would have been Radicians and the rest support people. There would have been 6 USAF or RCAF military officers (Data Controllers) depending upon whether the station was on US or Canadian soil.

The Aux Sites, of which there were 27, were also 25 modules long but there was only one of them. So, your world was reduced to being 400 feet long by 28 feet wide. The initial planned staffing levels for the Aux Sites was to be 12 people most of whom would have been Radicians.

The smallest station in the DEWLine world was the I-Site. They were a mere 5 modules wide and intended to house 5 people, one of whom was the Radician. Your world was now reduced to 80 feet long and 28 feet wide.

The radar, communications, and other technical equipment at the Main and Aux site were the same and that's where the 24-hour monitoring of the sky (surveillance) took place. As a Radician assigned to one of these stations, your job, in the early years, consisted of both maintaining the electronic equipment as well as doing Console duty monitoring the radar scopes, 4-hours on, 4-hours off. In later years, separate Console Operators where hired.

The I-Sites were a different animal. They consisted of four high-power Doppler transmitters, two facing East and two facing West. As the Radician assigned to an I-Site, your job was to keep the transmitters operating 24-hours a day. Of the four transmitters, two were always on-the-air (one to the East, one to the West) and the other two transmitters were "hot" spares ready to take over in an instant.

When you elected to join the DEWLine world you did so for a minimum of 6-9 months at a time. Despite the attractive renumeration, that was not everyone's cup of tea. Not everyone wanted to live in such small physical worlds, or to be away from

Photo showing the FOX Main module trains and overhead bridge.

their loved-ones or civilization for that long a time. Some left the Line well before the end of their contract and in a very few cases, some went crazy. I was involved on one such incident.

Chapter 3: Getting Hired

It was in the late 1950s when Canada's prime minister at the time, John Diefenbaker, said to the youth of the nation, "Go North, young man." So, being young and somewhat naive, I went.

I don't remember if I found the advertisement or if my mother brought it to my attention. The newspaper advertisement was for electronics technicians to go north to the Distant Early Warning Line for a salary of $1,000 a month plus all living expenses and end-of-contract bonus. Training provided.

Today, $1,000 a month doesn't seem like a lot of money, but in 1960 it was a lot of loot. Adjusted for inflation, a $12,000 a year income in 1960 would be the equivalent of over $102,000 in 2018. Not too shabby, as at the time I was making just shy of $230 a month or $2,750 a year as an electronics technician working at the National Research Council (NRC) in Ottawa.

I took time off work to travel to Montreal to the offices of the Federal Electric Corporation (FEC) where I was interviewed and given a technical test that I promptly failed. As a newly minted, 19-year-old electronics technician with two years of work experience, I knew nothing about radar.

Although I was only 19, I had been dabbling in electronics since the age of ten and had built most of my own radio equipment. I got my amateur radio (ham) licence, VE3EBF, in 1957 after passing the technical exams. At the time, these exams were a lot more stringent than they are today. By the time I went to technical school, I had already built up a good part-time business repairing radios. It appeared that I had a natural flair for electronics.

So, undeterred by my initial failure, I returned to Ottawa and went to the NRC technical library where I borrowed a couple of books on radar and studied them until I felt confident enough to take another shot at the FEC exam.

This time I passed the exam. Either that or they were desperate for technicians. Whatever, I was offered the job as an electronics radar technician, known as a Radician. The employment contract was for 18 months, the first three months of which would be spent training in the US before being sent to the Arctic. You were allowed a two-week vacation after nine months on the Line, after which you would return north for the remaining six months of your contract. Any subsequent contracts were 12 months in duration with a two-week holiday at the 6-month point. I was to learn later that, at 19, I was the youngest Radician to ever be sent north to the DEW Line up to that time.

Now I had to go back to NRC and resign my position there. I was working in the Structures Laboratory (M-14) maintaining a huge digital computer known as FERUT. While I didn't realize it at the time, it turns out that FERUT was the first commercial digital computer sold in Canada and the second in North America. It had originally been purchased from the Ferranti Company in the UK by the University of Toronto, hence the name FERUT, and had been used for research at the university until being acquired by NRC. I assisted in the final stages of the installation and was tasked with keeping the beast running.

At the university, it had been used to design the first automated traffic light system in North America, as well as being used for research studies for AVRO's Arrow jet fighter, one of the world's most advanced aircraft, and probably still would be if the development program hadn't been shut down and all six-prototype aircraft destroyed.

FERUT had over 4,000 vacuum tubes and its own 1400-cycle generator to power up the filaments and the rest of the unit. Whenever I powered it up in the morning, a tube would blow somewhere and one of my jobs was to find out which of the 4,000 tubes had decided to die. I had gotten to the point where I'd get into work early, turn the beast on, boot it up, and then go for breakfast at the NRC cafeteria. By the time I got back and started the testing processes, the tubes were all toasty warm except for the quitter. I'd troubleshoot down to the section level and then feel each of the tubes in the section until I found the cool one. Very technical, but hey, it worked.

You can find out more about FERUT and my adventures with it at www.FERUT.ca.

As I was one of the few people who knew enough about the computer to be able to keep it running, NRC was loath to see me go. During the exit interview, the gentleman from personnel offered me a 10% pay increase if I would stay. Ten percent isn't too bad and would have raised my monthly salary from $239 to over $250. When I told him that my new employer was going to pay me $1,000 a month, he looked stunned and said, *"Surely you jest?"* When I told him that it was true, that they were going to pay me four times what he was offering, he simply wished me good luck and we parted company.

End of exit interview and start of a whole new career adventure.

Chapter 4: The Adventure Begins

Getting Trained

The adventure began by having a medical and being informed that I would have to have my four, perfectly healthy wisdom teeth removed because they weren't about to fly me out of the Arctic if I had a toothache.

Now somewhat toothless (at least missing four big ones), I was off for twelve weeks of training in Streator, Illinois, a small-town south of Chicago. It was mid-March of 1960. There were 12 of us, as I recall, but I can only remember one fellow's name, George Sicotte, who lasted just a few months on the Line before calling it quits and I never saw him again. We were billeted in the Columbia Hotel, a somewhat seedy hotel that was dubbed the Tiltin Hilton. It had definitely seen better days...much better days. Or as someone noted, it was well past its "best before" date. Most of the guys had to share a room, but I was assigned to a closet-sized single room of my own at the back of the building, complete with a bed and sink. None of the rooms had toilets and most didn't have a sink, so we all shared the floor's common bathroom facilities. Very fancy! It was more like a rundown rooming house than a hotel.

The first course was a week-long weather observation course as one of our functions in the Arctic was to act as weather observers. For some strange reason, this was the only course that was mandatory to pass. If you failed this course, you were on your way home.

The technical courses were, well, technical. If you failed two of the weekly Saturday morning exams, the axe fell, and you were on your way to a new career. The passing mark was 70 percent and not everyone survived the 12 weeks of training. Being a young, eager beaver, I studied my butt off and passed all the exams.

While none of us needed a reason to drink, passing the Saturday exam usually sparked a celebration on Saturday night, giving us Sunday to recuperate. Some of us celebrated more than others. One of those people was a fellow classmate by the name of Reg something or other.

Reg was one of these people who wore thick glasses without which he couldn't find the nose on his face with either hand. Very, very early one Sunday morning, Reg's roommate found him huddled at the base of the shared toilet. Apparently, Reg had been out drinking, a lot, and he had been talking to Earl-on-the-great-white-phone. The roommate noticed that Reg didn't have his glasses on and asked him where they were. Reg pointed into the toilet which was filled with an interesting brew. Not wanting to lose Reg's glasses, his roommate screwed up his courage, rolled up his sleeve, and dipped his hand into the mess trying to find the glasses. It was at this point that he saw the glasses lying on the floor behind the toilet.

Reg's roommate told us later that he thought his arm was going to rot and fall off. I told him that if it had been me, I would have used Reg's arm to root around in the soup. Reg survived, but barely.

Middle of Nowhere

The training was held at a prototype DEWLine station in the middle of a cornfield about twelve miles outside town along Highway 17. We were transported to and from the site each day in a blue military bus with US Air Force markings. Very fancy, indeed!

Note: Apparently the site was decommissioned in 1982 and the property was sold to the farmer whose land surrounded it. The radome had been disassembled and stacked behind one of the buildings. According to DEWLiner Ed Groelle, who revisited the site in 1992 and again in 2010, the compound was now being used for storage. There were turkeys inside the fence, and sheep grazing in the area.

I remember the first time I saw the radar console. I noticed a control on the panel labelled "Anti-Jam Control," and I thought great, no one can jam the radar. Little did I know at the time that all the control did was lower the sensitivity of the radar receiver, which not only minimized the jamming but also the radar's ability to see any targets.

Apart from learning all about the technical equipment and how to repair and maintain it, we also had to learn how to track and report targets. Federal Electric engaged a local pilot to fly around at night to give us something to practise with.

The Streator Airport was a grass strip and was home to the local flying school which owned a Piper J3 and a derelict Cessna T-50 Bamboo Bomber. This is where I got my first taste of flying small planes. I ended up with about ten hours of flight instruction, as well as rides bummed on the nocturnal practice flights. I wasn't to take up flying again until the mid 1970s.

Streator was not what you'd call an exciting place. It certainly wasn't a hotbed of social activity. I have no idea as to what its claim to fame was beyond serving the local farming community. There was no discernible industry. The town's few restaurants served simple but good food. The most popular restaurant was a place called Rokey's and it was hopping on Saturday night, or at least as hopping as any place in Streator was, which wasn't saying much. Essentially, Rokey's was the local watering hole for the community. There was also a bowling alley that served beer, which made bowling a whole lot more fun than it was in Canada where drinking in an establishment like this was forbidden.

One weekend, one of my other team members and I decided to get out of town for some excitement, so we rented the town's only rental car and drove west to Kankakee. When we arrived, the whole town was eerily dark and quiet. We went into one of the local taverns to find it all lit up with candles. I thought, how quaint, only to discover there was a city-wide power outage. This didn't seem to interfere with our ability to drink, however.

On the return trip, I was doing the driving and my drinking buddy turned on the car radio and promptly went to sleep. After a short while, I turned off the radio, so it wouldn't disturb his sleep. I then followed his example by also falling asleep...while I was driving. Fortunately, the rumble of the tires on the side of the road woke us both up before we went into the ditch, and we survived the adventure unscathed.

It turned out that while I had turned the radio off so he could sleep, he had turned it on so that I'd stay awake. What we had here was a failure to communicate.

Northward Bound

Upon completion of the training, we were issued airline tickets to our embarkation points for the journey north. I was to leave from Montreal.

It was late July 1960, when I was issued with my US Air Force blue Arctic clothing at the Nordair hanger in Montreal's Dorval Airport and prepared for the long trip north to Hall Beach in the North West Territories as it was then known (now called Nunavut).

The flight the Hall Beach was via Frobisher Bay, now known as Iqaluit, the capital of Nunavut, and would take about 6-7 hours to Frobisher and another 2-3 to Hall Beach. We flew in a Nordair Douglas DC-4 CF-IQM. Interestingly enough, CF-IQM is still flying today (2018) in Buffalo Airways livery, some fifty-eight years later.

Travel was anything but fancy. No flight attendants and no hot meals, just a box lunch while you sat amongst the cargo. Cargo had priority over passengers in terms of space allocation. One was left with the feeling that the cargo was somewhat more important to the folks up North than we were.

Our Arctic gear consisted of a set of heavily lined coveralls with zippers from bottom to top, a parka with a huge hood with real fur trim, thick boots with removable liners that could be used in place of shoes, and mitts with fur backing. The fur backing on the mitts was used to wipe your nose which would run continuously when the temperature got to -20C or so. The problem was that the snot on the back of the mitts would freeze and it would feel like you were wiping your nose with rough sandpaper.

Before we took off for our northern adventure, we all made a pact that we would put money in a pot and the last person to cut off his beard would get all the loot. This fast road to instant riches was dashed when we arrived at our destination and were informed that beards were not allowed, as they might interfere with the seal on the Scott Air Packs that would have been used for firefighting. Apparently, the no-beard rule was relaxed in later years.

A Barren Land

So, in July 1960 at the tender age of 19, I found myself near the top of the world above the Arctic Circle as a civilian radar technician (Radician) on the Distant Early Warning Radar Line (DEWLine), ready to stand watch over the North American continent, ready to sound the alarm in case of attack by the Soviet Union. It was all very exciting for a young man.

I remember being tired and excited when we landed at Hall Beach, also known as FOX Main. The airstrip was at the Lower Camp about a mile and a half from the main buildings and you could easily see the huge white radome in the distance.

We all piled into the blue US Air Force bus for the trip to the Upper Camp. In addition to us newbies, there was a fair number of people who were returning from R & R (rest & recreation) leave, as well as some long-timers who were returning on a second or third contract.

As the newbies, we were somewhat shunned, as though we hadn't yet earned the right to call ourselves DEWLiners.

I don't remember much about those first few days apart from quietly celebrating my 20th birthday on August 4, 1960, at Hall Beach, 125 miles inside the Arctic Circle.

I was ultimately assigned to the Aux-site at Pelly Bay, code-named CAM-4, and was awaiting transport for several days. Finally, the day came, and I was thrown into a DC-3 along with a few sacks

of mail and some movies for the two-hour lateral flight west to
CAM-4.

Auxiliary (Aux) Sites

As previously mentioned, the typical Aux-site was made up of series
of 28 by 16-foot buildings called modules, connected side-by-side.
The result was a "module train" that was 28 feet wide by about 400
feet long.

I only have a vague recollection as to the layout; however, I
was able to find the following description by Clive Beckmann on the
Internet.

Module 1: Storage area

Modules 2 – 4: Diesel generators for power generation and hot
water for heating

Module 5: Electronics workshop and power mechanics office

Module 6: Transmitter Room

Module 7: Receiver Room

Module 8: Surveillance Room (Radar Console) and
Communication Centre

Module 9: Radar Room. The first 9 modules, known as the
Electronic Modules, were accessible only by Radicians and the
Station Mechanic using a keylock system.

Module 10: Station Offices

Module 11: Firebreak

Module 12: Receiving Room for incoming goods

Module 13: Walk-in Freezers and Incinerator Room

Module 14: Kitchen

Module 15: Dining Room

Module 16: Recreation area where movies were shown

Module 17: Recreation area containing pool table, bar and
Emergency Radio Room

Module 18: Transient Sleeping Quarters

Module 19: Firebreak

Module 20: Laundry Room, Darkroom, Potable water
Module 21: Bathroom and Septic Tank
Modules 22 – 25: Sleeping Quarters, 4 bedrooms to a module.

The module trains were built on pilings that were driven into the tundra below the frost line so that the whole building sat about four or five feet above the frozen tundra.

The base of the radome that held the radar antennas was 50 feet above ground and located directly over the Radar Room module. The rigid radome itself was 25 feet in diameter and contained the two AN/FPS-19 antennas, an upper beam and a lower beam, mounted back-to-back.

In addition to the main module train, each Aux-Site had a garage and warehouse. There were usually several abandoned Jamesway huts (long, half-round tents with a rigid frame and a canvas cover) that were left behind from the construction years. During the summer months, these tents could be used to house the extra workers that arrived each spring to do major outside work on the site.

Depending upon the time of year, an Aux-Site had a complement of between 12 and 40 people. There were some 10 to 15 in the winter months and more during the summer when construction and outside repairs were being done. Of the complement, 7 to 9 were Radicians, if we were lucky.

Upon my arrival, I was treated as the outsider I was until I was befriended by one of the other Radicians by the name of Tom Billowich. It appears that no one on the station cared much for Tom, and I became his one and only friend. I suspect he glommed onto me when I first arrived so that he could reserve me as his personal friend.

I learned later to be wary of people on the DEWLine who were looking for instant friendships. They were usually extroverts who were going batty amongst a bunch of introverts who didn't mind

Photo of CAM-4. My first home away from home.

being along. (The DEWLine is an introvert's heaven.) These extroverted people seemed to come fully equipped with a number of quirks that caused people to want to keep them at arm's length.

However, for whatever reason, Tom and I got on well together and I had a number of adventures with him, the last of which was a misadventure and saw Tom leave the DEWLine for the last time.

Rudy Hubner was the CAM-4 Station Chief. He was a fine gentleman and went on to become Station Chief at FOX Main where our paths would cross again. The Lead Radician was a short fellow by the name of Gaetan Chapeau, who always seemed to have a chip on his shoulder. We used to call him Napoleon behind his back.

The chef was a crazy Frenchman by the name of Red Chenil. Our paths were destined to cross several times during the three years I was on the DEWLine. He was an excellent chef, if a bit strange. He used to jokingly threaten me with a butcher knife from time to time. I think he'd been up north a bit too long.

So, CAM-4 was where I cut my teeth on the DEWLine. Because I was a bit of a technical nerd, I was keen on learning everything I could about the equipment at the station. Although we were capable of looking after all the electronic gear, we were often assigned to specific types. I was assigned to look after the air/ground and vehicular radios as my specialty. I was also responsible for maintaining the radio system that was used to communicate with the Intermediate stations (I-Sites) on each side of our site.

There were two Collins VHF air/ground radios systems, consisting of a 242F3 transmitters and 51N2B receivers, one for the general aviation frequency of 122.2 Mhz and one for the emergency frequency, 121.5 Mhz. These radios were used primarily for communicating with commercial aircraft. We also had two UHF air/ground radios systems, consisting of an AN/GRT-3 transmitter and AN/URR-35 receiver, for communicating with military and Strategic Air Command (SAC) aircraft on 236.6 Mhz as well as monitoring the military emergency frequency of 243 Mhz.

The radio system that was used to communicate with the two I-sites was a General Electric model VO-38 VHF system which ran about 250 watts, as I recall.

Our vehicles all had a AN/VRC-19 radios installed in them. We used the VO-38 to communicate with the vehicles. This meant that whenever we called a vehicle, the signals were also picked up at the two I-Sites which tended to annoy them.

I was also responsible for the LF beacon which was a Wilcox 99C also known as the AN/FRT-37.

Each station was equipped with an Emergency Radio Room containing a Collins 431B1 1000-watt transmitter, 74A4 receiver, and a three-element beam antenna. This room was at the opposite end of the module train from the main electronic modules, in one of the Recreation Modules so that in case of fire, it might be spared and used to summons help.

Federal Electric had a training program where a Radician could take technical exams on the various pieces of equipment.

Photo of the air/ground transmitters I was
responsible for maintaining.

There were five levels of proficiency with a Level 5 (called a Five-level) being the best. I quickly became a Five-level on the equipment for which I was responsible. Being a bit of a technical nerd, as I mentioned earlier, coupled with the fact that we didn't have a lot of things to keep us busy, gave me the time to delve in-depth into the various pieces of electronic equipment we were responsible for. By the time I left the DEWLine in 1963, I had attained a Level 5 proficiency in five different equipment categories, something that had never been done up to that time (1962).

Chapter 5: Story Time

What follows are over forty "adventures" that I either took part in, was a party to, or observed. They are presented essentially in chronicle order, as they happened to me. At least to the best of my recollection.

"Adventures" is pushing the poetic license envelope a long way. These are "events" that happened to me that provide insights to what is was like to live and work on the DEWLine, hopefully told with humour. And hopefully for your enjoyment.

The Fishing Expedition

I mentioned earlier that I had several adventures with Tom Billowich. I call one of these adventures the fishing expedition.

It was one of those rare days off that we occasionally got, and Tom convinced me that we should walk the six miles down to the airstrip and do some fishing for Arctic char. Our chef, Red Chenil, would have been delighted to cook up anything we caught for us and if there was any left over, we could share it with the other station personnel.

Six miles is a bit of a hike, so when I protested the long walk, Tom said we could take a shortcut via the old road. Besides, the people at the airstrip could give us a drive back, Tom said. So, we got the station's fishing gear and off we went.

We were about halfway to the airstrip via the old road when I noticed the people driving up the main road back to the station. So much for our ride back... I was starting to be an unhappy camper.

We finally got to the lake by the airstrip. Tom was the first to cast his line. It went out about 15 feet and came to an abrupt stop. That was all the line he had on his reel. Hardly long enough to reach the water. No problem. I still had my rod and reel and it looked pretty full.

I'm not a fisherman, but being game to try things, I cast my line with all the vigour I'd seen other fisherman display. Out the line went...and then it just kept on going. No one had attached it to the reel! Both Tom and I watched as my hook, line and sinker went flying out over the lake to disappear forever.

The Arctic char were safe for a while longer. It was a long, quiet, six-mile, uphill hike back to the station. I didn't talk to Tom for a few days and I've never been fishing since.

Saturday Night in the Arctic

Officially, we weren't supposed to have any hard liquor on the sites. Every spring, the sealift and airlift would bring up large quantities of beer for general consumption. We were allowed to purchase six cans of beer a week. I didn't care much for beer, and still don't, so I'd sell my six cans off to the highest bidder. I never got rich, but it gave me spending money for other sundries.

In any event, despite the supposed lack of booze on the sites, each station had a well-stocked bar. Whenever anyone when south for their R&R leave (a two-week rest and recreation vacation), they were tasked with returning with a suitably large quantity of booze. Other bottles came by mail, some inside loaves of bread, many just well packed as gifts for the long journey. Basically, Saturday night was escape night and some people escaped farther than others. One such escapee was a Radician by the name of Brian Webb.

Brian didn't just like to drink, he liked to get smashed. This didn't usually cause a problem except on Saturday night, or more importantly, on a specific Sunday morning when he was supposed to relieve me from my Radician duties.

It was a typical Saturday evening at CAM-4 and the station personnel were gathered in the recreation module areas enjoying a few drinks and games of pool and cards. I had to go on duty at midnight, so I was drinking pop while most of the others, including Brian, imbibed the devil's brew.

The evening festivities carried on well after I went on shift at midnight, and every now and then I dropped down to the recreation module to see how things were going. What wasn't going was Brian. He wasn't going to bed. I mentioned to him that he was to relieve me in a few hours and he might want to get some sleep. My pleas fell on deaf ears and a sodden mind. I was getting annoyed.

On one of my trips to the recreation area, I carried on to my sleeping quarters, which happened to be across from Brian's. I have no idea what possessed me to do what I did next. I got a tube of shaving cream from my room, went across to Brian's room, found his toothpaste and carefully transferred a slug of shaving cream from my tube into his toothpaste tube, after which I went chuckling back to work.

Eight o'clock in the morning came, but Brian didn't. Nine passed, then ten. Finally, at around 11 a.m., a bleary-eyed, dishevelled, somewhat-still-drunk Brian appeared. As he mumbled a good morning into my face, I caught the smell of booze, bad breath...and shaving cream. I asked him if he had shaved his teeth that morning. He looked at me quizzically, mumbled something, and plopped himself down in front of the radar console. I went off to bed.

It was later in the day when the final act of the play happened. I was sitting in the toilet when a now-sober Brian appeared holding his toothbrush and tube of toothpaste. Oh no, I thought. This can't be happening before my eyes as I strained to see through the crack of the toilet door. It was, it was. He was going to brush his teeth!

It only took a few seconds, but now that he was sober, Brian could now taste the shaving cream. It wasn't a pretty sight, so I'll spare you. I enjoyed every minute of it.

Of course, Brian accused me of putting shaving cream into his toothpaste tube, but I denied any knowledge of it. In the end, he was never sure enough to take revenge on me.

But I was very careful about where I hid my own toothpaste until I left the site.

Movie Time

If we hadn't already watched them, Saturday was usually movie time, as well. When the weather cooperated, we'd receive three movies a week on the weekly lateral flight that also brought us our supplies and, more importantly, our mail.

The movies were shown in the recreation module, using a 16mm projector. Each film usually had three reels, and we'd have to stop between reels to refill our drinks while the projectionist set up the next reel for viewing.

As a rule, these were first-run movies and were well received by the station staff. However, apparently someone at head office in Paramus NJ had overspent the annual movie budget and we started to get some real dogs. When that happened, it usually got people shouting and throwing things at the screen as the evening wore on. I remember one such dog of a movie called "Carthage in Flames," which was so bad that we all had problems following the storyline. Characters on the screen would race their chariots from the right to the left and then back again, over and over. It was so confusing that at the end of the first reel, when the projectionist missed the second reel and put on the third one, no one knew until the closing "The End" appeared on the screen. At first, we all thought it was just a (thankfully) short movie. We didn't understand the movie anyway and only discovered the un-played second reel as we were packing up this dog for shipment to the next site.

As an avowed Introvert, I preferred working the evening or night shifts as I enjoyed the relative quiet of the station during those quiet hours. After I got off the evening shift one Saturday I decided to watch a movie on my own. It was about 2 a.m. My shift-mate had gone to bed and all the rest of the station was sleeping, except for the two other Radicians who were working the overnight 12 to 8 shift.

The movie was Alfred Hitchcock's "Psycho." I didn't know who Hitchcock was or that he made horror/thriller movies, so I was blithely watching along what I thought was a mystery movie when I got to the part where Janet Leigh is in the shower at the Bates Hotel, semi-naked (which really caught my interest), when all of a sudden the shower curtains get pulled away and there is Anthony Perkins slashing away at Janet Leigh with a huge knife. Blood was spurting everywhere. It was at this point that the reel ended. There I was, absolutely horror-struck, sitting in a darkened room, alone, thinking, what the hell was that?

I'll tell you, that movie had a profound impact on me. I don't think I took a shower for months, and when I did, it was during the day. Colour me young and impressionable.

Christmas at the Real Pelly Bay

Father Vandeveld had been in the Arctic longer than I had been alive. This venerable gentleman had spent over twenty years in the Arctic, most of them at the Pelly Bay Mission. He was to give me my most memorable Christmas ever and one that has never been topped.

CAM-4, Pelly Bay, is located about ten to 12 miles north of the Pelly Bay Mission that Father Vanderveld called home. You could always tell when people from the Mission visited the station because they only had to be in the building for a few moments before the air circulating system alerted us that either the Eskimos* from the Mission had arrived, or someone had left a dead seal in the entranceway.

(*Note: While I refer to "Eskimos" in this document, the politically correct term for the indigenous people of the North is now "Inuit." I'll continue to use the term Eskimo as that was what I knew them as. The word "Eskimo" was not a derogatory word. Of course, they are fine people and I mean them no disrespect.)

One such visit brought with it an invitation to visit the Mission on Christmas Eve to join in the festivities. A group of eight or ten of us accepted, and on the appointed day we all climbed into the Bombardier snowmobile (Snow Pig) and drove to the Mission.

There were approximately 120 Eskimos living in and around the Mission at that time. What they had done in preparation for the occasion was to build four fairly large igloos in a square, placing them some 30 feet apart from each other. They then built a huge igloo using the four smaller ones as corner pieces. They completed the structure by removing the now interior walls of the four small igloos, leaving a huge 50-foot round igloo with four small alcoves.

All 120 inhabitants of the Mission were in the igloo that evening. A mass of humanity for Christmas Mass. They sang and played games. They had a piñata-like object hanging from the top of the structure, and all the Eskimo children had an opportunity to be blindfolded and to try smacking it with a stick. When one of the children did finally hit it, all manner of treats rained down on the spectators.

As strangers and visitors, the people from CAM-4 stayed in the background, observing and enjoying the simple pleasures of the event. It was a touching and moving experience.

On the return journey to the station in the snowmobile, one of the Eskimos offered me a frozen "treat." I thanked him, and as I munched on the treat and it began to thaw in my mouth, I realized that it was a piece of raw frozen fish. I don't like raw fish.

To this day, I'm not a big fan of sushi (raw fish), but whenever I have the opportunity to taste some, I'm transported back to that quiet evening many years ago and remember Christmas at the real Pelly Bay.

Christmas at CAM-4

After the Christmas Eve at the Pelly Bay Mission, the Christmas dinner at the station was a less emotional affair. To the company's credit, they really tried to give us a bit of a Christmas feast. They had formal menus printed up, and the chef prepared special fare for the occasion. It was a very pleasant evening, and everyone partook of the meal, including the on-shift Radician who was assigned to maintenance duties. The only station member absent from the festivities was the Radician who had the Console duty.

Until I had worked my first Christmas Day at CAM-4 I had always considered that day to be a special holiday. It was while watching the radar go around, around, and around that I realized that there were many people, and I was one of them, for whom Christmas was just another day of the year. There were lots of people from airline pilots to police and fire personnel to bus drivers to whatever that were busy at work and not with their families.

It was at that moment that Christmas lost its magic and simply became another day of the week. In later years, when I was volunteering on the phone lines at the Ottawa Distress Center, I would often work Christmas Day to give some other volunteer time to spend the special day with their family.

Drag Racing

Entertainment opportunities 120 miles inside the Arctic Circle are few, so when I had a chance to learn a new "trade," I leapt at the opportunity.

In order to keep our airstrip useable, it wasn't ploughed, it was dragged. We would tie a huge log or bar about 20 feet long and drag it crossways up and down the airstrip using a D-8 Caterpillar.

In one of my bouts of boredom, I got the Lead mechanic to show me how to drive the D-8 and drag the strip. If I thought my job watching the radar was boring, this was the pinnacle of boredom and the mechanic was delighted to suck me into doing this mindless job.

I found it mildly interesting for the first couple of hours, after which it just became hard work. The actual driving up or down the strip wasn't such a big deal but getting the beast of a D-8 turned around without fouling the trailing log was a challenge.

So, while it wasn't exactly drag racing, dragging the strip helped pass the time and served a useful purpose. If we didn't keep the strip in good condition, we wouldn't be receiving any aircraft.

No aircraft meant no movies and, more importantly, no mail. In the end, I didn't exactly consider myself a heavy equipment operator. I only did it once. Too much fun isn't good for a person.

The Case of the Missing Scotch

Some people shared their booze with others willingly, while others shared less willingly or even unknowingly. Here's what happened to Albert's bottle of scotch.

I don't know why Albert Lemaire coveted his bottle of scotch, but he did. It was as though it was an Aztec treasure to be displayed and talked about but never to be touched by others. If Albert had simply kept his mouth shut, he might have had a chance to enjoy his scotch.

Albert was a Sector Electrician and travelled from site to site doing esoteric electrical repairs that the station mechanics either didn't, couldn't, or wouldn't do. He'd been at CAM-4 about ten days and no amount of cajoling or convincing could get him to share the pleasures of the bottle's contents. We even offered to buy it off him but to no avail.

It was early on an uneventful Saturday when a dastardly plot was hatched. Albert was due to leave the next day and was down at the airstrip doing his electrician thing when some of the station crew decided to liberate the scotch. We weren't going to steal it; we were going to borrow it.

We found the bottle tucked away in Albert's bunk, and using a razor blade, we carefully cut the seal around the screw top. We then transferred the contents to another bottle and refilled Albert's bottle with a scotch-looking fluid made of tea.

As a final touch, we resealed the top, using some clear scotch tape so the bottle would crack as it was "opened" sometime in the future.

That Saturday evening when we were all sitting around the bar/lounge area, one of the guys "discovered" some scotch behind the bar and offered it to everyone, Albert included. It was a grand evening. Everyone was getting pleasantly potted on Albert's scotch, including Albert.

The next morning, some of us slightly the worse for wear saw Albert off as he crawled aboard the plane for the short hop to CAM-D (aka Simpson Lake), the I-site to our west. We waved Albert and his bottle of tea goodbye and silently went back up to the station.

It was a couple of days later when the radio channel from CAM-D came alive with some of the bluest language I've ever heard. Apparently, Albert had opened his bottle of scotch only to discover that tea doesn't taste anything like scotch. We turned the volume down and let Albert rant.

If only Albert had kept quiet about his coveted scotch. Little did I know that I would be following Albert to CAM-D soon.

Missed Boogie (Target)

As you might imagine, our primary mission wasn't to visit, fish, watch movies, or play practical (and non-practical) jokes on one another. There was a much soberer side to our existence and we took it extremely seriously, Console duty.

This was to be Tom Billowich's last adventure. It was a quiet Arctic night. But then most Arctic nights on the DEWLine were quiet. Tom and I were halfway through the midnight to 8 a.m. shift. It was Tom's turn to man the console, so I went off to do some preventative maintenance routines (PMs) on the air/ground transmitters in the Transmitter Room.

It was somewhere around 4:15 to 4:30 AM when all hell broke loose. We received a call from FOX Main to do an immediate Minimum Discernible Signal (MDS) test on both beams of our FPS-19 radar system. There was no mistaking the sense of urgency. I called the console and asked Tom what was up. "There's something wrong with the radar," he told me, "We missed a target."

I hot-footed it to the radar room and did the tests. No problem. The radar was just fine. What was going on? I went back to the console room where Tom told me that both CAM-3 and CAM-5, the stations on each side of us, had reported the target but we weren't "painting" it (seeing it on the radar screens). I looked at the right-hand screen of the console. We were sure as hell painting it now. What gives?

I asked Tom what was going on. All he would tell me is that we missed the bogie and he was now in deep doo-doo. He denied dozing off. I sent him off to do another MDS test for himself and he returned to confirm my earlier results. There was nothing wrong with the system. He really was in trouble.

There was a lot of mental and physical hand-wringing on Tom's part as he continued to claim that he hadn't fallen asleep and that there just had to be something temporarily wrong with the radar.

Before the end of the shift, we were informed that Tom should gather all his belongings up and be ready for pickup later in the day and taken to Fox Main.

Radar console at FOX-Main, with Paul Kelley on duty. This is the same type of console that Tom apparently fell asleep at.

Tom not only gathered up his things but gathered up his thoughts as well. By the time he was being driven to the airstrip for pickup by the venerable old DC-3, CF-IQD, he was prepared to present a vigorous defence in an attempt to salvage the situation and his job. I shook his hand and wished him well.

Tom never got an opportunity to present his case. They took him off the lateral flight and put him directly on the southbound flight, out of the Arctic, and out of a job.

Technical failures aside, there was simply no acceptable excuse for missing a target. Tom missed the bogie, and, in the end, we missed Tom.

Working in the Dark

One of the things that helped seal Tom's fate was the cameras that were mounted on the radar receivers in the radar room. As soon as a radar target triggers an alarm, the cameras are supposed to photograph one full sweep of the antennas. The system didn't always work as advertised, but it did in Tom's case and the resulting photo showed a target.

Each Aux and Main site had a fully equipped darkroom, and if you knew what you were doing, you had free use of all the supplies to develop your own films and photos. In fact, you could use the darkroom even if you didn't know what you were doing, and that was the case in my situation.

At the time, no one at CAM-4 was particularly interested in developing film or even learning how. Always up for a challenge, I volunteered to be the station's resident darkroom specialist.

Before long I was mixing chemicals and developing my own black and white films, as well as printing as many photographs as I wanted. Ultimately, I even expanded my talents into developing colour slide film. I had to purchase the chemicals from the south as the stations were only equipped to deal with black and while film.

Still, it was a great way to learn darkroom techniques at absolutely no cost. Hell, I could use an 8 x 10 sheet of photographic paper just to do test shots!

Other Talents (or lack thereof)

I didn't limit my experimenting to just photography. I branched out into barbering.

As a general rule, the station chef was the person who cut hair, at least at CAM-4 it was. Our chef was a crazy French Canadian by the name of Red Chenil and who was a couple of knives short of a full set.

You knew that you were in Red's good books when he picked up a butcher knife and threatened to kill you. For some reason, Red took a shine to me and often threatened to cut off various parts of my body. Maybe it was because I was always practising my French swear words on him.

In any event, Red also doubled as the station barber and did a real good job. As with any skilled practitioner, Red made cutting hair look relatively easy. I mean, if someone who specializes at hacking sides of beef apart with a butcher knife can cut hair, surely someone with my finely-honed soldering skills can also cut hair. Or so I thought.

My opportunity to test out my hair cutting skills (or lack of same) came about quite innocently.

It was the summer of 1961 and CAM-4's population had swollen by the addition of a construction crew who were working on the airstrip and other construction projects that could only be done in warm weather.

There weren't enough sleeping quarters in the main building to house the newcomers and they had to bunk down in the old Atwell tents that were still on the site from the early construction days.

Although housed away from the main building, they always had their meals with us in our dining module.

One evening I was sitting across from a young construction worker and we struck up a conversation during which he asked about how he could get his hair cut. Being adventuresome, I ventured that I could do it for him. I managed to avoid answering any questions about my barbering experience until later, when it was too late. We agreed to meet later that evening in the laundry area which doubled as the barber shop.

Everything went along fairly well, in that I was able to seriously reduce the amount of hair the fellow had on his head. It was the finishing touches that caused the problems.

The best way to explain what went wrong is to use the analogy of trying to level a wobbly dining table. First you cut a bit off one leg and test it out. It's still wobbly but in a different direction now, so off comes a bit of another leg. You keep repeating the process of taking a bit off one leg after another until eventually you end up with a coffee table that is, unfortunately, still wobbly.

Well, the hair cutting sort of went the same way. A little off the left, a little off the right, and then repeat the process. It was during this finishing touch that the fellow asked me how many haircuts I'd given. Not being one to lie, I confessed that this was my first one. There was a noticeable increase of tension in the laundry area.

I continued with the trimming. I think maybe his ears were not on straight. That's the only reason I can give for why the haircut turned out looking so bad.

Frankly, I can't remember too much about how the session ended; I just remember it wasn't good. In fact, I decided that I was best to work the night shift until he left the station. I did catch a glimpse of him the next day. He was wearing a sweater with a hood (a hoody) that he was using to hide my handiwork. I don't blame him.

I was keeping a pretty low profile so I'm not sure how it all worked out. I suspect that Red took pity on the fellow and did his best to repair the damage.

I didn't come out of hiding until the fellow left the site for the last time a few weeks later.

No Days Off

I mentioned earlier that a full complement of Radicians was seven to nine people. This number gave you enough Radicians for three, two-person shifts a day and still allow you to have a couple of days off a week. Losing anyone can create problem. Losing Tom Billowich from CAM-4 because he missed a boogie created a major problem because we were already short-handed at that time.

We then went through a period of several months where we worked seven days a week, week after week, without any days off. Not that there was much to do on your day off, but it's tedious working day after day without any end in sight.

At one point, this tedium was matched by a long spell of bad weather where we couldn't get any supplies airlifted into the station for 28 days. The food was beginning to run low and tempers were running high. While we didn't get to the point of looking at each other as possible sources of protein, the main freezer got pretty empty. If it got much emptier, we'd have had to send the station Eskimos out on a hunt for food. No mail (particularly no letters from loved ones), no movies, and no booze made for a group of very grumpy people.

It's not that they didn't try to get in to us. The Nordair pilots who flew the lateral DC-3's were a hardy bunch from the old bush pilot school of flying. They knew only too well how important their flights were to us, particularly when there was mail onboard.

Every now and then the weather would look promising, only to have it close in by the time the aircraft arrived overhead. It was incredibly frustrating for the people at the airstrip to hear the DC-3 trying to land but ultimately having to go back to FOX Main with our mail and movies.

There was dancing in the streets (a figure of speech only) the day the plane was finally able to land. The very first thing we all wanted was our mail as this was the main connection to the rest of the world for most of us.

Calling Santa Claus – Adventures of VE8SK

I was fortunate enough to have another way to stay connected with the outside world in addition to receiving letters from home. It was also a great way to relieve boredom. As the only amateur radio (ham) operator on the station, I had the use of the station's Emergency Radio equipment which was a Collins 431-B1, 1500-watt transmitter, and a Collins 75A4 receiver, along with a three-element beam antenna. All excellent equipment and a radio amateur's dream station, with the one exception being that the beam rotor usually froze up during the winter months. We always made sure it was pointing south when we shut down the radios.

My radio call sign while I was in the Arctic was VE8SK or Victor Echo Eight Sierra Kilo. However, around Christmas time I'd go on the air as Victor Echo Eight Santa Klaus and I'd have ham operators lined up a mile deep to let their children talk to Santa's station in the north.

It was great fun to spend my off-duty time "Ho, Ho, Hoing," and talking with eager young voices from all over North America.

Whenever possible I'd use the radio equipment to allow personnel to talk to their families through the use of other ham radio operators who had a device known as a phone patch. For non-technical, non-hams reading this, a phone patch was a device that connected a radio to the telephone lines and provided the ability for the ham at the southern receiving end to patch their radio into the phone line and then call a person and allow them carry on a conversation with the person on the other end of the radio link, i.e. at the DEWLine station.

So why was this so important? In the early years of the DEWLine, when a person went north, it was generally for several months (or longer) at a time. There was no telephone links, no television to watch, no daily newspaper to read, and no radio to listen to. Basically, there was no connection with the south at all beyond the weekly mail delivery (weather permitting).

We were extremely isolated. At the smaller I-Sites there may be as few as 4-5 people. On an Aux-Site you may have 15-25 people depending upon the season and on a Main Site there could be between 50 and 150 people depending upon the time of year. Inter-site communications didn't exist except for the technical people and even then, they were generally limited to talking to the stations on either side of their station.

All this meant that the ability to talk with ones loved one, especially at a special time like a birthday, anniversary, Christmas, etc., was very important. Even though the conversation was in simplex mode (only one person could talk at a time), hearing a loved one's voice after months apart was a treasured moment.

Whenever I could make a solid connection for a station member with their loved-ones in the South, I was a hero.

While no longer the "hero," I still dabble in amateur radio to this day and hold the callsign VE3UU (as well as my original callsign, VE3EBF).

A Woman's Voice

Another service that was appreciated by station personnel was when we patched our air/ground communications into the station's PA system. Especially when we were able to get an airline stewardess (as they were called back then) from an overhead flight to talk with us.

Once a week, Scandinavian 935 from either Vancouver or Calgary, I'm not sure which, would pass overhead en route to Amsterdam. On more than one occasion, I'd ask the pilots if it might be possible to have a chat with a stewardess. The pilots knew that we were in the middle of nowhere, keeping an eye on their progress, so out of appreciation for our services, they often accommodated us.

I was able to accomplish this feat during Christmas Day, 1960, when most of the station personnel were indoors relaxing. I patched the stewardess's voice through the PA system to all the modules and we had a very pleasant conversation for some ten minutes until I ran out of things to ask her.

The sound of a woman's voice to a bunch of guys who have been away from civilization for too long is like music. We had a short but nice symphony that day.

Escape from the North

When it came time to go out on my first R & R leave at about the nine-month point, I declined as I knew that if I went out then, I'd never come back. The thought of another seven- or eight-month stint up in this wilderness was just too much to bear. So I elected to stay on for another three months and left after a year on the Line.

I had another problem before going south—my weight. When I arrived on the DEWLine some 12 months earlier, I weighed in at about 120 pounds, soaking wet. Due to the great food and sedentary lifestyle, I now weighed 150 pounds. A weight, by the way, that I wasn't to see again until I was in my late sixties, and then only fleetingly!

Not only that, but my apparel had been reduced to one pair of pants and a red shirt that I loved with a passion. Every two weeks, whether they needed it or not, I'd run them through the washer and dryer. I'd sit in the laundry area in my underwear, reading a book, until they were done.

My beloved shirt had a number of rips and tears which I had repaired with masking tape. I'd put the masking tape on the inside so it didn't show. I would have used the ubiquitous Duct tape but I don't think it had been invented yet.

All in all, this was not the best clothing to go south in, so I measured myself up, found the Sears catalogue, and ordered a three-piece suit for the princely sum of $29.99, including a second pair of pants.

Of course, I also bought a couple of shirts and a pair of shoes as well. Now I had my "going-to-town" clothes and was ready to tackle the south. Frankly, I don't think I looked particularly dapper, but it was the best I could do under the circumstances.

Not Much Pay

The company had an arrangement to send your pay directly to the bank; however, you could have them send you a cheque every two weeks so that you had some spending money. Not that there was much to spend it on. I elected to have a dollar a day sent up, so every two weeks I'd get a company cheque for 14 dollars.

There are not a whole lot of things to buy on the DEWLine. I didn't drink beer, so I sold my beer allotment to the highest bidder, and I didn't know how to gamble, so when I went south on R & R, I had 26, 14-dollar cheques to cash. When I told the teller at the bank that these were my paycheques, she sadly commented that I didn't get paid much. If she only knew!

Being Bushy

I had been living in a 400 X 28-foot world with 14 other people for a year by this point and it took a while to get acclimatized to the hurley-burley of civilization again. Basically, I was in a condition we called "bushy" or out-of-touch. If I was in a room with more than five or six people, I'd begin to feel claustrophobic and have to get out. If I wanted to get to the other side of the street, I'd simply strike out across the road, totally oblivious to the traffic. More than once I almost got knocked into the next life. It's an odd feeling of being totally disconnected with the here and now.

One of the highlights of my vacation was a trip to Chicago to visit the Museum of Science and Technology, where I was able to wander through the World War II German submarine

U-505 and watch the move of its capture during the war. It was a great place to visit if you were technically or scientifically minded. I also checked out the Cleveland School of Electronics which had a pretty comprehensive correspondence course on advanced electronics. I signed myself up for the course and used it to educate myself further, as well as pass the time on the Line.

If the museum was one of the highlights of the vacation, an incident with my mother was a definite low point. It probably comes as no surprise, but when a bunch of guys are forced to live together in close quarters for prolonged periods of time, their language can go to pot, to put it politely. As I recall, on the Line, about every fifth word out of a person's mouth was the famous "f" word. I mean, it got to the point that you didn't even realize you were saying the word, it just came out.

So, you can imagine my mother's horror when, at breakfast one morning, I asked her to pass the f**king butter. She hauled off and hit me across the face. Stunned, I asked why she'd hit me. When she said, "Don't use that kind of language with your Mother," I asked, "What f**king language?" She hit me again. I instantly figured it out and I quickly learned to be a lot more careful about what came out of my mouth while I was down south.

Apart from insulting my Mother, I managed to survive my R&R and returned to the DEWLine, this time via Winnipeg as TransAir had won the contract and had replaced Nordair on the North/South trips. I was all refreshed and ready to complete the last few months of my first contract.

Returning North

The flight from Winnipeg to Hall Beach was somewhere around 12 hours. Twelve boring hours. In an attempt to minimize the pain of the trip, someone suggested that it would be a good idea to get drunk before climbing on the aircraft and thus sleep for the majority of the trip. It sounded like a pretty good idea (at the time), so I bought a 16-ouncer of rye and promptly got stupid drunk.

I don't remember getting onto the plane, but I do remember waking up a couple of hours into the flight and being deathly ill for the remaining ten hours of the trip. I didn't attempt that trick ever again.

Time to Move On

I had been at CAM-4 for over a year at this point, so when I returned from my R & R it was time to move along to a new adventure.

Being a Radician on one of the Intermediate Sites (I-site) was not a desirable position. First off, it was a lonely existence as the station had a normal personnel complement of only three to five people: a Station Chief, the Radician, a mechanic, a cook, and a couple of Eskimo workers. Usually either the Radician or the mechanic held the position of Station Chief. As you were the only technical person on the station, you couldn't really leave the building too far or for any length of time as you had to be available 24 hours a day to deal with any equipment failures.

I'm not sure how I got sucked into going to CAM-D (Simpson Lake) which was located between CAM-3 (Shepherd's Bay) and CAM-4 (Pelly Bay). I think it was the promise of being considered for a position on the coveted Sector Crew after I served a term at the I-site. The Sector Crew was a group of semi-elite technical people who travelled from station to station across the sector, solving problems that the site personnel couldn't solve or providing additional assistance as needed.

However, it came about, I found myself at this tiny station, truly in the middle of nowhere. Its most prominent feature was its 300-foot tower that held the Doppler antennas that pointed west toward CAM-3 and east toward CAM-4. It stuck up like a sore thumb on a frozen cadaver.

As you drove up to the main building from the airstrip, you passed the two Eskimo houses and the original Jamesway huts that were used by the construction crews during the building of the station. One of the huts still held the site's NDB radio beacon that I was ultimately to move to the main building.

The I-site's main building made the Aux-site look like a palace. It was constructed of five of the 28- by 16-foot modules, side by side in a mini-module train, all mounted above the frozen tundra on four- to five-foot stilts or pilings.

As before, my memory is hazy on the layout of the building, but I found some information in an article by Martin Allinson, who spent far too much time on I-sites in Dye Sector in the early 1960s. The following is his description of the building layout:

Module 1: Generator Room containing two 20 KW diesel generators.
Module 2: Electronics Module containing the four Doppler radar transmitters.

CAM-D Main building

Photo of a typical, 5-module I-site, plus garage.
Home for up to five people.

Module 3: Station office, Radician's bed, Dining area, Kitchen, Bathroom

Module 4: Dormitory and main entrance door

Module 5: Storeroom

The building was entered through the main door in Module 4. There was a small corridor about 12 feet long that joined into the main passageway that ran through the whole length of the building.

Module 5, which was to the left as you entered the main passageway, was devoted to storage for food, spare clothing, and so on, and a large water tank.

Turning to the right at the main passageway, you had a cage that contained the 60 Hz motor, 400 Hz generator sets and a big sewage tank on the right and the dormitory on the left. The dormitory contained three double bunks and was the sleeping area for the mechanic, cook, and any winter visitors, such as members of the Sector Crew.

You entered the "living module" (Module 3) through a fire door. On the right, up a few steps, was the bathroom and shower. This took up one quarter of the module. The other quarter on the right was the kitchen area with a water heater, stove, sink, cook's table and a washing machine for doing your laundry.

On the left of this module were the station chief's bed and his desk, the dining table, and the Radician's bed (with the radar equipment alarm by his pillow).

Module 2, the electronics module, contained the four radar transmitters to the left and the Radician's workbench, storage shelves, desk/communications centre to the right.

Module 5 held the two 20 KW diesel generators, but thanks to good soundproofing, the noise level wasn't excessive.

What I've described here was the layout for CAM-D. On some of the other I-sites, the entrance door was on the other side of Module 4.

I can't remember the name of the Radician I replaced at CAM-D, apart from the fact that he disappeared on the next available aircraft after familiarizing me with the four FPT-4 transmitters, the electrical power switching panel, and the Gonset Air/Ground radio.

He couldn't get out of there fast enough.

Working Around the Clock

I arrived just in time to partake of the annual resupply airlift. This is when all the POL (Petroleum, Oil and Lubricants) supplies for the whole year are brought to the station. I don't know how many hundreds of 50-gallon drums of diesel fuel we received for the generators, but they all had to come by aircraft. They usually used the venerable C-46 Curtiss-Wright Commando aircraft. The C-46 probably had about three times the cargo capacity of the Douglas C-47 (also known as the DC-3) which normally flew the route year-round.

Even with three times the payload, it took almost two weeks of continuous flights to resupply the station. The aircraft flew 24 hours a day, and while they had extra pilots for the aircraft, we were on our own. I literally slept at my desk by the air/ground radio in the electronics module. I would be awoken every couple of hours with the arrival of another plane. Only bad weather gave us any break from the endless grind. (At one point they flew in one of the new Radicians to help with the air/ground duties which gave me some respite.)

The rest of the station crew, with usually included a few extra people for the summer, had to unload the barrels from the aircraft, and drive them to the main site where they unloaded and stored them. Then they repeated the process over and over again as each aircraft arrived.

Lesson Learned

Bill Wands, an electrician and genuinely nice person, was the Station Chief when I first got to CAM-D. Bill, along with Lyall Lalonde, the Sector Mechanic, assisted me in removing our NDB radio beacon transmitter from one of the Jamesway hut/tents and moving it up to the main building where we had to install it in the electronic module.

We had to dig down into the tent to get at the door in order to remove the transmitter. It had been quietly operating, unattended, for several years. We then laid it on a sled and dragged it to the main building with a bulldozer. Once the transmitter was installed in the electronics module, I had to climb the 300-foot tower to connect one end of the new antenna to the top of the tower.

CAM-D's 300 foot tower, 1961

By the time I managed to climb the 30 storeys to the top, my legs were like rubber. Then disaster happened. As I reached over the edge of the tower to connect the wire using a nut and bolt, the nut slipped out of my hand and fell 300 feet to the ground. I suspect it continued going 300 feet into the tundra!

Stupidly, I had only brought one nut and bolt with me. Now all I had was a nutless bolt. There was nothing left to do but climb down the tower, grab a handful of nuts and bolts, and climb the tower again.

By the end of the second 300-foot climb, even my leg muscles had muscles and they were screaming in agony. I learned a valuable lesson that day and always made sure I carried spares of everything I could whenever I had to do stuff like that again.

Doctor Brian

Being the only Radician on an I-site meant that you were also the first-aid person as well.

The Eskimos at CAM-D lived about a half-mile away, halfway between the airstrip and the few modules that made up the station. One of the Eskimo women was with child, pregnant so to speak, and was growing subtly larger with every passing month. As she usually stayed in the Eskimo quarters, she was generally out-of-sight and out-of-mind. She became top-of-mind one evening when her husband brought her to the main building complaining of stomach cramps. Stomach cramps? How about labour pains? First-aid training notwithstanding, I was not prepared for this!

What to do? The first challenge was communication. The Eskimo, whose name I've long forgotten, didn't speak very good English and I sure as hell didn't speak Eskimo. No one seemed to know just how long the lady had been pregnant or when, exactly, she was due to give birth.

I immediately rummaged around our limited library and found what I was looking for, the St John's Ambulance First Aid Manual. I opened it to the index and looked for "emergency childbirth." There it was. I was saved. I quickly opened it to the emergency childbirth section and here's what it said:

1.   Make patient comfortable.
2.   Call a doctor.

Yikes! This I didn't need. The closest doctor was in FOX Main. I immediately got on the radio to CAM4 and had them patch me through to FOX Main, where I tried to locate the doctor. Time stretched on forever as I waited for my saviour to call.

Finally... a call from CAM-4. They had the doctor and were patching him through to me. He asked me how far along she was. I told him I didn't know. He asked if she was dilated. I didn't know. Hell, I was only 21 and had never really looked at these things before!

He finally gave his advice. If it was a boy, I should tie the umbilical cord with a blue ribbon and if it was a girl I was to tie it with a pink one. I went ballistic.

I told the doctor, in no uncertain terms, that they were to send a plane, now, either to take her or me out of here. I didn't mind changing klystrons but I hadn't signed up to deliver babies.

After I calmed down, they agreed to send a plane, and eight hours later my Eskimo friend was winging her way to FOX Main and competent medical help. I'm sure that both of us were breathing a lot easier.

Postscript: It turns out that she really did only have stomach cramps and gave birth to a healthy baby girl about three weeks after her evacuation from CAM-D.

The Dancing Washing Machine

It was a big day at CAM-D. We received a new washing machine to replace the one that had died several weeks before.

Now, washing machines were no big deal, unless you were without one for several weeks. By this time, some of our clothes weren't just standing up by themselves; they were walking around looking for some fresh air and begging to be washed.

We got the thing off the plane and into the back of the 4 x 4 truck for the one-mile trip to the main site. The Eskimos wanted the packing case for something, so they quickly spirited the material away, never to be seen again, leaving us to manhandle the heavy, commercial-grade unit, into the building.

We squeezed the unit through the doorways and into the kitchen/eating area module where we placed it approximately where the old machine had been. We were all anxious to give it its first workout. While the cook prepared the final touches to supper, we put in our first load. A really big load.

It was while we were all eating around the small table that the trouble started. All of a sudden, the machine went into its high-speed spin cycle and literally took off, dancing and hopping around the room. The imbalance of the wet clothes in the drum had turned this normally docile machine into a mechanical bucking bronco. After the initial surprise wore off, three of us jumped on top of the machine to try and contain it before it did too much physical damage to the facilities.

There we were, all three of us, hanging on for dear life as this killer washer tried to buck us off and trample us. It just kept on dancing and bucking for what seemed forever until it finally moved far enough that the power cord came free from the wall outlet and the machine, thankfully, calmed down.

As we surveyed the damage, we realized while we had put the machine *approximately* where the old machine had been and not *exactly* where it had been. There were concrete blocks in the way.

In our zeal for clean clothes, we had forgotten that the old machine had been mounted on these blocks. Now we knew what the blocks were for. They weren't to just raise the machine off the floor as we had thought; the added weight was there to keep the machine from dancing away with our clothes.

No one said much as we unloaded the machine, mounted it on the concrete blocks, and went back to finish a cold supper with the new washer humming gently in the background.

King of the Northwest Mounted Police

It was like a scene from a bad movie. There I was, not knowing what to do when King of the Northwest Mounted Police, in the form of an RCMP constable, showed up at the door and saved the day.

It started earlier that evening. As I mentioned before, as the only Radician at CAM-D, I doubled, hesitantly, as the first-aid person. One of the site Eskimos, Peter Nakoolak, brought his four-year old daughter, Emily, up to the main modules with a crushed finger. Apparently, little Emily had gotten her finger caught in a door and basically squeezed it enough that it had broken open at the top.

Albeit small, it was a pretty nasty-looking wound. In cleaner southern climes, it might not have been too much of a problem; however, having seen the Eskimo quarters, I was afraid of Emily getting an infection and losing her finger or perhaps her hand.

According to the station's St John's Ambulance First Aid Manual, I was to give her a shot of penicillin. OK, but where? I had three ampoules of penicillin and a needle, but no instruction as to where to inject it.

I'd always gotten my penicillin shots in the butt. However, as I was never watching when it happened, I wasn't sure exactly where in the butt to stick it. This is when King of the North arrives on the scene.

Emily Nakoolak. CAM-D 1961

Now picture this. I'm located about 120 miles above the Arctic Circle, some 50 to 70 miles from the nearest Auxiliary site, and 250 miles from a doctor who wasn't available anyway, when there's a banging on the module's main door. In walks this RCMP constable who had just parked his dog team—yes, a dog team—in front of our building, and he wants to know if he can bed down for the night with us. Is this out of Hollywood, or what?

Photo of the RCMP officer and his dog team.
Pre-SkiDoo era!

I welcomed him with open arms because I knew that RCMP personnel have extensive medical and first-aid training. I quickly explained my mini-medical emergency to him and he took charge. He gave the shot to Emily, bandaged her finger, and calmed her down.

Another life saved in the nick of time by King of the North.

I was to have other medical adventures with Emily over time, including helping her with a bout of impetigo, which is a rash that can be quite uncomfortable. Emily's mother and father were Margaret and Peter Nakoolak and I came across them several times as I travelled around this part of the Arctic.

As a footnote to history, in 2007 someone saw the picture of Emily that I had posted on my personal website and I received an email from Emily's sister, also called Emily. Apparently, the Emily I had known had died sometime after I left the Line and this lady had been named Emily as well. Emily #2 had never seen a picture of her sister. She told me that both her parents, Peter and Margaret, were still alive and living in Inuvik, NU.

And now for the rest of the story... . A few years ago I was contacted by a social worker who was working with the Nakoolak family to find out what had happened to Emily-1. Emily had fallen ill and was flown out to Winnipeg for treatment where she died. Apparently, the family was not informed of Emily's death for some long time and Emily's remains were never returned to the family, nor were the whereabouts of Emily's remains disclosed to the family. The family was struggling to put closure on this part of theirs and Emily's life.

Hospitals generally keep good records, so I suggested that the social worker contact the various Winnipeg hospitals and asked them to search their records for an Emily Nakoolak, age 10.

I don't know how this story finally ended but I'm saddened that any system could treat indigenous, or any people, in such a cavalier fashion.

No Rest for the Wicked

Intermediate sites were situated between two Auxiliary sites and transmitted signals east and west which were picked up at the Aux-sites. It was a Doppler system and was intended to fill the gaps between stations. In fact, it was called a Gap Filler System. The theory was that should an enemy aircraft try to sneak between the two Aux stations, the transmitted signal would be disturbed, and an alarm would go off at the console at the relevant Aux station.

Theory is one thing and practice is another. Any number of things would cause a false alarm. One of those many things was a noisy transmitter at the I-site, so it was not uncommon to get a call from one or both of the Aux-sites at any time of the day or night to go check the FPT-4 transmitters.

If the call happened to come in the middle of the night, you had to get up and go tend to the electronic beasts in the electronic module. This usually meant switching over to the standby transmitter and then tending to its errant brother.

Because the Radician shared the sleeping and living module with others, if you were up all night, the only place you could sleep during the day without being disturbed was in the midst of the electronic gear. At least it was toasty warm in the electronics module and the drone of the diesel generators in the next module helped put you to sleep.

The whole gap filler radar system was from an earlier era and fraught with false alarms to the point that many of the console operators would simply ignore the alarm or turn off the console displays altogether. They finally turned off the system for the last time and closed down the I-sites in 1963/4.

Now That's Cold!

I've been outside in minus 50-degree F weather in a shirt. Not for long, mind you, but I wanted to see what it was like. Frankly, it was cold! Interestingly enough, it didn't feel cold until the wind hit you, then you felt the cold deep inside. It felt as if someone had slashed you with a razor. It was an odd feeling.

It was at CAM-D where I did my first scientific experiment: the famous disappearing water act. There is a temperature at which, if you throw warm water into the air, it virtually disappears. I'll admit I didn't start out to do a scientific experiment; it just turned out that way.

I was in the electronics module one evening and the rest of the crew were in the living module watching a movie. As usual, the movie screen was set up against the door to the electronics module. As I didn't want to disturb the gang just because I had to take a whiz, I went through the generator module and stepped outside into the minus 50-degree F weather and quickly relieved myself.

When I went outside the next morning there was no evidence of my having relieved myself. The urine had simply evaporated into thin air. Now that's cold!

Another small step for mankind.

A Time Management Lesson

Our station chief, Bill Wands, was whisked away one day and replaced by Ray Dawes. Ray was to teach me a lesson that I still use to this day.

Ray was a mechanic. He was a big man with a gentle disposition, who didn't much care for the paperwork involved in the job. With every lateral flight came a ton of paper that had to be dealt with. I'd watch Ray wade through the piles, reading this, noting that, and throwing away a fair amount of the stuff, as well.

One day, while watching Ray sifting through the crap, I noticed that one of the messages he threw away was a message from his boss requesting him to do something or other. I asked Ray why he threw it away. He replied, *"If it is really important, they'll send it again!"*

Interesting philosophy! Ray would mentally log in the first request and would only take action after he received a second (or third) request. What a time-and work-saving technique! Apparently, it worked well because Ray never got into trouble and went on to be the Station Chief at the FOX-3 Aux-site where he did an excellent job.

I was to use that time management, work saving, technique to my advantage many times over the years!

Time to Move Along Again

My contract had come to an end and it was time to leave CAM D and go out for my EOC (End of Contract) leave. My first contract was up in November 1961. Fortunately, or unfortunately, we were short-handed, so when I offered to delay my EOC leave, it was well received, and I stayed on for several more weeks, working over the 1961 Christmas period, before returning to civilization again. As a reward for my "generosity" of helping out during the Christmas period, I was allowed six weeks rather than the normal four weeks for my EOC leave.

By now I had some decent going-to-town clothes and I was much more careful with what came out of my mouth as far as swearing was concerned. As such, I had a pretty good holiday, with the exception of disappointing my mother yet one more time.

Like most moms, mine had kept my bedroom ready for my ultimate return (the return of the prodigal son). When I told her that I had rented an apartment for the six weeks so that I could be on my own, she wasn't a happy camper. I didn't mention to her that I had high hopes of running a den of iniquity. She was crushed that her only son didn't want to spend his hard-earned holiday sitting with his mother. While she ultimately got over it, I don't think she every truly forgave me for my heartlessness.

One of the additional problems of being the only (and therefore favourite) son of a proud Mother is that she was forever offering my technical services to her friends. Your radio doesn't work? No problem, my son will fix it for you. Broken toaster? Bring it over for Brian to fix. Television on the fritz? Brian will take care of it.

I didn't want to spend my vacation time repairing people's rejects, so I finally had to tell her that I didn't repair TVs, radios, or toasters anymore, and that if her friends had any radar sets or high-powered transmitters that needed looking at, I'd be delighted to help out. She wasn't too pleased. She thought I had a bad attitude. Mothers!

In all fairness, my mother was a wonderful person who always believed in me and felt that I was a genius when it came to electronic stuff. I was about 15 or 16 before I came to the disappointing realization that I wasn't a genius (damn!) but just a guy who was handy with his hands and who had an affinity for electronics.

Here We Go Again

Upon my return to the Line, I got the position on the Sector Crew that I had been promised. Because of my technical background, I was assigned to look after the air/ground equipment on the sector's six stations.

Being a Sector Radician was a bit of a lonely existence. For the most, part you were an outsider upon arrival at a station and treated as such. As an introvert, I wasn't bothered too much by this. Once you were there a time or two and demonstrated that you were more of a help than a hindrance, you were adopted by the station or at least tolerated by them.

I did manage to make a spectacle of myself during a first visit to one of the sites. I had just come from a site that had a terrible chef. Not only was the food badly cooked, it was always cold or lukewarm at best. I was to the point where I'd just pop whatever it was into my mouth and swallow it as soon as possible.

So, imagine my surprise when I sat down for supper at the new site and popped a searing hot chunk of potato into my mouth. I severely burned my tongue and the roof of my mouth before, to everyone's horror, I spit the thing back onto my plate and jumped up. I'm not sure but I think I might have used the "F" word a time or two. What a wonderful first impression I must have made.

As Sector Crew, you had to travel with all your possessions which you would throw on the plane moments before you got thrown on along with the sacks of the all-important mail and the movies. In the overall scheme of things, the movies and mail were understandably rated more highly than the Sector Crew was.

Movie Time (Part 2)

After being shown at the Main station, movies were always sent to the most westerly station in the sector and would work their way across the sector from west to east. If I was travelling from station to station, east to west, I'd end up missing every second batch of movies. On the other hand, when I was travelling from west to east, I'd get thrown on the plane along with the movies, and both the movies and I would be off-loaded at the next station. This meant that I'd get to see the same movie for several weeks in a row. Not many of the movies were worth seeing more than once, but when you're desperate you'll watch almost anything. Sort of like watching television today!

God's Will

Because I got the opportunity to work on the same air/ground equipment at every station, I got to know the technical idiosyncrasies of the various pieces of gear. One such idiosyncrasy almost got me in hot water with one of the company field inspectors from the head office in Paramus, NJ.

These inspectors would arrive on your doorstep from the south and follow you around to ensure that procedures were being followed and that the work was being done properly. They tended to leave you alone for the most part, but every now and then you'd get an eager beaver who knew it all even though they knew very little. (I was tempted to say they knew nothing but that would be unkind.)

The Collins VHF receivers that I worked on had a particular bias measurement that simply never met the specifications that were outlined in the preventative maintenance schedules. After checking and rechecking all 18 receivers in the sector, I kept getting the low reading. The maintenance schedule called for a value of at least -5 VDC at a particular test point and I could never get anything better than about -4.5 or so.

One day I was being shadowed by a HQ inspector who was watching my every move. When I got to this particular test point, I noted the low value and was about to move on when he stopped me and asked what I intended to do about the low reading. I showed him that the other two receivers on the station also measured low and that I'd found the same low value all across the sector. He was a bit confounded by this phenomenon and wondered what we should do about it.

Having already tried every technical trick I knew, and the receivers were all working fine, I had come to the conclusion that the specifications were in error and not the receivers. He didn't seem too keen on accepting that explanation, so out of frustration, I said, "Maybe God wants it that way."

Of course, I was just kidding, but little did I know that this gentleman was extremely religious and took my comment quite seriously. He furrowed his brow and pondered the comment for a moment or two and then made the observation, "Maybe you're right." Problem solved, subject closed. Or so I thought.

Unfortunately, it didn't solve my problem because the inspector assumed, incorrectly, that I was a potential "believer" and he wanted to pursue the saving of my soul. I didn't catch on to this for a while because, being young and curious, I was interested in religion, and in the beginning, I was comfortable chatting about the subject. I got increasingly more uncomfortable as the fellow increased the pressure on me to go to a quiet part of the station and "kneel with him in prayer."

At this point I began to realize that the situation was getting out of hand and I tried to wind down the topic without much success. He was due to move along to another station when a bizarre event occurred.

I rejoiced when he took off for the airstrip. I was free, or so I thought! Strangely enough, the aircraft ran into mechanical problems and had to return to the station. He immediately sought me out and told me that God had brought him back to the station for a particular reason and it became quite clear that I was that reason. Having no idea how to cope with the situation, I started working the overnight shift and hiding out in order to get away from the fellow.

He finally had to go on with his mission, both technical and religious, and I learned to be a whole lot more careful when discussing religion and politics.

The BOPSR Club

As a member of the Sector Crew, I didn't really have a place to call home. The members of the Sector Crew were usually constantly on the move, going from one station to another across the sector, looking after their assigned group of equipment. As mentioned, we were usually thrown on the plane right after the movies and mail and got off the plane immediately after them.

If we had a home, it was the BOPSR Club at FOX Main. Named after one of the many reports (Building & Outside Plant Status Report), the BOPSR Club was a single leftover module that sat, all by itself, about 200 feet from the main module trains. It had electricity, a space heater, some eight to ten bunks, and that's about it. Oh, it had one other thing. It had a urinal of sorts, but more about that later.

Whenever members of the sector crew were in FOX Main, we stayed in the BOPSR Club.

As it was rare for the whole crew to be at FOX Main at the same time, the bunks were often used by personnel coming up from the south while they waited lateral transportation to their assigned sites. Sort of a transient quarters.

Newcomers to the Line who stayed in these less-than-posh quarters were easy prey to the old-timers who, in exchange for the newcomer's booze, would spin tales of life in the north.

Back to the urinal. As the module had no washroom facilities and as it was a long, cold, 200-foot walk to the main building, some enterprising soul had built an enclosed veranda-like addition through which he stuck a metal funnel so the men could relieve themselves without freezing anything. The funnel had a hose that ran to a 50-gallon drum. This wasn't a problem in the winter when everything froze very quickly, but in the summer months when this drum thawed out, we all stayed on the road and away from the club. Not a pleasant aroma for a while.

It was the winter of 1962. I and a couple of other sector crew members were between trips and hiding out in the BOPSER Club when we were blessed with a couple of newbies fresh up from the south and bearing gifts (booze).

I rarely drink unless it's there and if it's there I drink. It was there and I drank. Every now and then, one of us would get up and go use the urinal in order to make more room for the booze. I don't know about you, but the more I drink, the drunker I get and the drunker I get, the sleepier I get.

On one of my trips to the urinal, I fell asleep standing up, and a part of my body, which will remain nameless, but which rhymes with the planet Venus, came in contact with the metal funnel. Anyone who was a kid in Canada, particularly of the male variety, knows that when a part of your body, your tongue for instance, comes in contact with frozen metal, you stick to it. That's what happened to me!

I awoke instantly to find myself attached to the funnel by my penis! What to do? I tried spitting to see if the warm saliva would free me from my bounds. No luck. Finally, I did what every young child finally does when they find their tongue stuck to the metal fence or pole, I pulled away, leaving a small part of me still attached to the metal funnel.

Fortunately, alcohol has an anaesthetic property that helped dull the pain. I've always claimed that, had this accident not happened, I would have been a danger to all womankind (don't I wish).

Another Kind of Freezing

I had yet another adventure with the cold that I didn't care much for. I was on a three-hour flight from FOX-3 (Dewar Lakes) to FOX Main when the heater in the DC-3 decided to quit. These heaters were cranky at the best of times and this was not one of the best of times. The outside temperature was in the order of minus 40 or minus 50 degrees Fahrenheit and the temperature inside the aircraft quickly began to drop to match those numbers.

I was in the cargo section of the aircraft, alone with the exception of a large fuel bowser that was also being transported to FOX Main. We were all supplied with Air Force Arctic survival gear, but even though I was all dressed up like an Egyptian mummy, the cold was beginning to penetrate my very soul, starting with my feet.

Not exactly first-class travel!

As time went by, the cold got worse and worse. It got to the point where my toes were hurting so much that I was crying involuntarily and praying for my feet to freeze solid and stop hurting. I was absolutely desperate. I'd never been so cold in all my life and I haven't been since.

The two pilots weren't in much better condition, although when one of them came back and suggested I come up to the cockpit, I discovered that they had a bit of heat from the engines. That was not a pleasant flight. My toes still burn whenever I think of it.

Going Crazy

I had been sent to FOX-3 to replace one of the Radicians who had gone looney-tunes.

No one knows just when Phil Collins went crazy but crazy he went, and I was designated to replace him.

People go off the deep end for many reasons, some psychological, some medical, some who knows? While I've always contended that you had to be a bit crazy to be a DEWLiner, the Federal Electric Corp took great pains to put DEWLine candidates through a series of psychological tests to weed out those who might crack under the strain of being isolated for long periods of time.

I had met Phil on a number of occasions as I travelled across FOX Sector as part of my Sector Crew duties and I liked him.

Apparently, Phil didn't drop off the deep end quickly; he slid into craziness slowly. It started with Phil complaining about the "little people" who were trying to get him. Other station personnel thought he was just kidding around. As the days went on, Phil's complaints got more and more persistent. Now the "little people" were coming up through holes in the floor of his room. He was beginning to see them in odd places. Toward the end, Phil took to carrying a carving knife from the kitchen to protect himself. The last straw was when they found Phil on top of the module train chasing the "little people."

Then two things happened. They put in an urgent call for a replacement and the weather immediately closed in.

I sat in the BOPSR Club at FOX Main for four days waiting for the weather to lift. Meanwhile, at FOX-3, they had Phil tied to a stretcher and had to let him shout and scream until he would finally tire himself out and fall asleep.

On the fourth day, the weather lifted enough to allow the mail and I to be thrown onto the DC-3 for the trip to FOX-3. It was a tense group that greeted us on our arrival. Phil was there, all bundled up in his parka, busily doing something. I went over and greeted him. He looked sane but had a slight faraway look to his eyes. I asked him what he was doing. He told me that he was trying to get the fluid out of his lighter and that you couldn't fly with fluid in your lighter. Okay, Phil, whatever you say!

On the return trip to FOX Main, Phil was seated next to a military person who wasn't familiar with Phil's condition. Phil asked if he had a razor blade. The guy found one in his shaving kit and gave it to Phil who promptly tried to cut his own wrists. Following a scuffle, the razor blade was taken away from Phil and he was restrained.

About this time, the weather at FOX Main closed in and the plane had to land at FOX-2 to wait it out. Apparently the "little people" had followed Phil and the personnel at FOX-2 were treated to a night of Phil's ranting.

They finally got to FOX Main and put Phil on the southbound trip to a hospital in Winnipeg. It turned out that Phil had tonsillitis and the infection had poisoned his system causing him to have delusions. Phil wasn't crazy, just sick. While I'm not sure, I believe Phil ultimately returned to the line to continue his duties as a Radician.

Meanwhile, I was given Phil's old room at FOX-3 and took over his duties on a temporary basis. Having a rather strange sense of humour, I complained about the holes in the floor of my new room and the little people. No one laughed.

The Ghost at the Airfield

While I was replacing Phil at FOX-3, I had another of my Arctic adventures. It was one of those things that simply weren't supposed to happen.

It was about 4 a.m. on a typical August morning. The overnight shift was unfolding as it should when it happened.

I had already finished my four hours of watching the FPS-19 radar in the console room and was busy doing maintenance on the air/ground radios when the console operator, my shift mate, called me to the console room.

I ambled in to the console area and asked, "What's up?" What was up was that the telephone at the old abandoned airport terminal building was giving an off-hook signal, but when we answered the line there seemed to be no one there.

The telephone relay on the 740 PBX just kept clacking away trying to make a connection. Clickity-clack, clickity-clack, clickity-clack, on and on it went. Who (or what) had removed this long, unused telephone from its cradle at the airport six miles away?

After much discussion, it was decided that a volunteer (apparently me) should go down to the airport and see what was up. So off I went in the USAF, blue 4 x 4 truck, bouncing my way down the dirt road to the airport.

As usual, the road conditions made for a slow trip down to the airstrip, giving my fertile mind far too much time to conjure up what might have caused the off-hook condition. It might be something as simple as the wind having blown the receiver from the cradle; or a polar bear ambling into the abandoned building and causing havoc; or worse, some axe-wielding lunatic, ready to trap and kill the first thing that walked through the door.

I have no idea where this axe-wielding lunatic would have come from, but he was alive and well in my imagination by the time I arrived at the terminal building, alone. I suspect it was my earlier adventure with Alfred Hitchcock's movie Psycho that may have done it.

Photo showing a typical 4X4 that we used on the
DEWLine in the early days.

The old and abandoned terminal building was located at the far end of the airstrip. Over the years, a small babbling stream had developed, separating the strip and the building.

There I sat in the 4 x 4, looking across the stream at the abandoned building with every blood-filled scene from every horror movie I've ever seen passing through my mind. Fortunately, I was a young man and hadn't seen that many horror movies, but I'd seen enough to let my imagination go wild.

So, with great trepidation, I climbed out of the 4 x 4, mud clinging to my boots as I forded the stream and found myself standing at the front door of the old airport terminal building. I tentatively pushed open the door and stood there looking at my shadow in the doorway as I tried to see into the darkness ahead. I chided myself for not bringing a flashlight along.

There was just enough light to see that there appeared to be no one there. He was hiding. I just knew it. I screwed up my courage and stepped into the building. So far, so good, I thought. As I glanced around the empty building it suddenly happened. The telephone rang!

I jumped so high that only the weight of my mud-caked boots kept me from hitting the ceiling or taking off like a scared jackrabbit. I'm sure my heart must have stopped for a moment or two.

I traced the source of the ringing and answered it. It was the console operator. Apparently, the off-hook condition had just cleared itself. He thought I had done something and was calling to see what I had done. Apart from almost defecating in my pants, I hadn't done a thing.

I hung up the telephone and took off as fast as my muddy boots would allow. As I drove back to the main building, I wondered once again, who or what had caused the off-hook condition. Now I know.

It was the ghost of DEWLiners past, waiting in the terminal building for the lateral flight to take them to FOX Main and the journey south.

Idle Hands (and Minds) at Play

While I was at FOX-3, I got into trouble for modifying the appearance of the helicopter that serviced FOX-C (Ekalugad Fjord) from FOX-3.

CF-HNG was a Sikorski S-55 helicopter operated by Okanogan Helicopters out of Vancouver and stationed at FOX-3. I can't remember the mechanic's name, but the pilot was Oli Sindberg. Oli and I got along pretty well, and he'd often let me ride along in the cockpit when he was doing his supply runs to FOX Charlie.

As you know, the sun is just below the horizon in the middle of the night in early July and it is quite bright out. It was midnight and Don Kerr and I had just finished the evening shift and were wondering what we could do to amuse ourselves. Like me, Don was a bit of a practical joker, so he enthusiastically embraced my idea to rechristen Oli's helicopter.

Armed with a roll of masking tape and a felt pen, we changed the Okanogan Airlines name on the side of the ship to "The Grace L. Ferguson Airline and Storm Door Company," after a popular Bob Newhart comedy skit. We adorned Oli's helmet with the name "Crash Sindberg" and relabelled several of the instruments in the cockpit with incredibly amusing names that I've long forgotten.

We then went off to bed in order to catch a bit of shut-eye, so we'd be fresh for when Oli and his mechanic saw our handiwork in the morning.

Oli was mildly amused, to put it kindly, but his amusement turned to annoyance when, as they removed the masking tape from the side of the helicopter, the paint also came off in big chunks. The result was a huge mess. Not enough of a mess to require repainting of the helicopter immediately, but it would have to be repainted the next time it went south for a major overhaul.

Without realizing how much it would cost, Don and I offered to pay for the repainting. Thankfully, our offer was refused and we quickly went about the job of correcting the damage as best we could.

I was able to repay the debt a bit by working on Oli's Automatic Direction Finding (ADF) radio, and in so doing, almost got myself killed.

Oli's ADF (Automatic Direction Finder) was very insensitive and once he flew five to ten miles from the station, he couldn't pick up a useable signal. As I was the local air/ground "expert," I offered to have a look at his radio for him. While I was the A/G specialist, I was more familiar with the "ground" part than the "air" part, but I didn't let that deter me from trying to help.

I don't remember if I had any schematics for his radio; however, I was astute enough to figure the thing out. In the absence of any suitable test equipment I suggested that Oli fly us out about ten miles where we still had a weak signal and then allow me to tweak the equipment that was located in the back of the passenger/cargo compartment.

So, on the next good day, Oli and I departed for parts unknown to adjust his set. I was in the passenger/cargo compartment with the door open and a pair of headsets on so that I could hear Oli and ultimately the ADF receiver. We were hovering between 200 and 300 feet above the tundra, and by doing my technical magic, I was able to make a noticeable improvement in the reception. I buttoned up the radio compartment and went forward and banged on the cockpit bulkhead to let Oli know that I was done and that we could return to the station. Oli banked the helicopter dramatically to the right and I started to slide toward the open door.

My heart leaped into my throat and only the wire on the headset and my wild grasping at the door edge kept me from falling out of the helicopter.

Was it an accident or was Oli trying to kill me for mucking up his helicopter? I still wonder.

The Top of the Mountain

Somebody figured that they had better get me out of FOX-3 before I caused any more havoc, so I was sent over to FOX Charlie I-site.

There was a problem at FOX-C. A large quantity of POL had gone missing and the Station Chief, Ray Campbell, was being hauled up on the carpet and investigated, and they needed someone to take over the station in his absence. So off I went to FOX-C as the Acting Station Chief for about a month or so.

FOX Charlie is located on top of a 3,400-foot unnamed mountain at the base of Ekalugad Fjord. During the summer sealift, supplies can be brought up the fjord and then trucked up a winding road to the station 3,400 feet above. I had heard stories of some vehicles that were brought in during the sealift and didn't survive the 3,400-foot trip. They burned out their engines before reaching the station. One of these was allowed to coast back down to the unloading area where it was pushed out on the ice the next winter, only to disappear into the fjord the following spring.

Most of our supplies had to come over from FOX-3 via Oli's helicopter, CF-HNG. Fortunately, Oli didn't hold any grudges or maybe he was just making up for trying to kill me, but he always did his damnedest to get our supplies to us, particularly the mail which we considered a critical item. The weather didn't always cooperate.
I
If the weather was good at FOX-3, it might not be good at FOX-C, and vice versa. One of the most beautiful phenomena I witnessed at FOX-C was when the fog would roll up the fjord 3,400 feet below the station. As the day wore on, the fog would rise until it

was level with the station and you almost felt you could walk across it to the other side of the fjord. A half hour later and the fog had continued to rise to engulf the station in a thick fog that limited your visibility to 20 or 30 feet. No helicopter on those days.

As I recall, I was there for six weeks before Ray came back and I resumed my Sector Crew duties and moved on. This time I was off to FOX-1 (Rowley Island, NWT) for my usual check of the air/ground equipment and my infamous polar bear hunt.

The Great Polar Bear Hunt

Quite frankly, polar bears are dangerous, very dangerous. They can scoop a 300 to 400-pound seal out of the water with one paw. They can also run across the snow at speeds exceeding thirty miles an hour. Consequently, whenever a polar bear started to hang around one of the stations, it was time for a hunting expedition.

Having polar bears hanging around the station was a danger to anyone working outside, including the Radicians who had to make trips to the Stevenson Screen where the wet and dry bulb thermometers were kept and where we had to go to take the hourly thermometer readings. No one wanted to be wandering around in the blowing snow and the dark if there were polar bears in the area.

Polar bear near FOX-1, 1961

It was a sunny afternoon when there was an announcement on the PA system that there was a polar bear at the kitchen firebreak area. Of course, we all grabbed our cameras and made a beeline for the door area. One of the lads opened the door and was facing a startled polar bear. Fortunately, the person who opened the door was less startled than the bear and slammed the door shut, and we all fell over ourselves trying to get away from the area. As near as we could figure, it was a fairly small bear and probably only weighed about 750 pounds. Big enough!

When we had all calmed down, the Station Chief called for the station's resident Eskimo and explained that he was to get his rifle and get rid of the polar bear. Only Eskimos were allowed to hunt polar bears in the Arctic at that time.

By this time, the polar bear was ambling down the road toward the station garbage dump, so we all went outside and followed it, getting as close as we dared and taking pictures. Finally, we piled into the back of one of the 4 x 4 trucks and followed the bear down the road. At one point, the bear went off the road to the left, so we stopped our vehicle, got out and started to follow the bear on foot.

By now the Eskimo had retrieved his rifle which turned out to be a single shot .22. I'm glad I didn't know at the time or I would have run the other way.

The Eskimo started taking shots at the bear. While this was all going on, it occurred to me that the bear was going to get annoyed at being shot at and might want to take his anger out on someone. Because I was closer to the bear than I was to the truck, I started to hot-foot it across the snow in the opposite direction.

While I was desperately trying to get away from the angry bear, I looked over my shoulder to see what was happening and saw the bear stumble and fall. The Eskimo then closed in to finish off the bear. It was a sad but necessary event. Then we all proceeded to have ourselves photographed with the dead bear as though we were the "great white hunter." I was photographing one of the mechanics kneeling beside the bear, holding the rifle, when the bear gave one last lurch. It was probably gas, but I wasn't taking any chances.

I took off in the other direction and the mechanic leapt up and tried to hand off the rifle to anyone who would take it. It was as though he was saying, "I didn't do it. I didn't do it. It wasn't me."

Foxes, Foxes, Everywhere

Both FOX-1 (Rowley Island) and FOX-2 (Longstaff Bluff) were almost overrun with foxes. They had beautiful white coats during the winter months. You could get close enough to feed them by hand which probably wasn't the wisest thing to do unless you had thick mitts on.

They would appear all over the place and lived under the modules until hunting season arrived, when they would all disappear. Not because they were hiding but because they were all caught by the Eskimos who would use the meat for food and the pelts for revenue.

The fur trade was alive and well on Rowley Island.

Becoming an Old Hand

It was time to go out on R & R again and I'd been across the FOX sector more times than I cared to remember. I'd been frozen, been chased by caribou, chased by a polar bear, and I generally felt that I had seen and done it all. At the tender age of 22, I was becoming an old hand, but I was also getting tired.

I had decided this was to be my last contract and I wanted off the sector crew. I was offered the position of Lateral Radician at FOX Main when I returned from R & R. I accepted the offer and went south for another adventure, this time in civilization.

Frankly, I don't remember much about my trips south. I know I had good times, spent a lot of money, drank a lot, and generally got myself recalibrated mentally. It was also the time when I met the lady who ultimately became my first wife and the mother of my two boys, Michael and Patrick.

One Last Time

For some reason, probably bad weather, the trip back north ended up at DYE Main (Cape Dyer) instead of FOX Main, so I and several fellow travellers found ourselves housed in a Jamesway hut at the DYE lower camp airstrip awaiting a lateral flight to FOX Main.

DYE Main's lower camp is about 8 miles from the main building and we avoided going up there in case we were pressed into service. So that meant we were stuck in this tent with not much to do. At some point we discovered that one of the travellers, who was new to the Line, had a huge bottle of Drambuie. I mean, this was a big sucker! I'm not sure how we managed to do it, but we convinced the fellow to share his snake-bite medicine with us, probably in exchange for inside information on how to survive on the DEWLine.

I'll tell you, it's one thing to have a liqueur glass or two of the stuff, but after a couple of water glasses full, everything, including the snake, dies. All of us woke up with incredible hangovers, only to be told to grab our gear and get on the DC-3 for FOX Main. It wasn't exactly a bunch of happy travellers who crawled onto the aircraft for the bumpy flight "home."

Home Again

I landed at FOX Main for the start of the last half of my second tour, some 25 months after I first arrived on the Line. I was older but I'm not sure I was a whole lot wiser. In any event, it was time to start a new position as the Lateral Radician.

The AN/FRC-45 tropospheric scatter system was the lateral radio system that connected each of the sites together and contained the 24 multiplexed communication channels that were used to transfer information back and forth across the Line. The system had to be "aligned" once a month and it was a big production requiring the efforts and coordination of a Radician at each of the Aux-sites. The Lateral Radician at the Main station was basically the orchestra leader for the event.

Because looking after the lateral wasn't too labour intensive, I was also assigned the responsibility of looking after the Model 755 PBX telephone switching equipment. The thing was full of stepping relays that were best left alone. While the preventive maintenance procedures required semi-annual burnishing of the relays, I soon learned that the philosophy of "if it ain't broke, don't fix it" applied in spades. As soon as you tried to clean the contacts with the burnishing tool, all manner of grief occurred. Calls stopping going through, calls were dropped, people were angry... I learned to let sleeping dogs lie.

Author aligning the AN/FRC-45 Lateral
equipment at FOX-Main.

The upside of working on the telephone exchange was the ability to pass the time eavesdropping on other people's conversations. Frankly, it wasn't all that interesting, but it helped ease the boredom. It was just my way of checking the "quality of the lines."

As a general rule, the Radician who maintained this system was allowed to work permanent days. After the "thrill" of learning a new set of technical gear subsided, and then getting thoroughly bored listening to other people's telephone conversations, I got set into a pattern.

Too set, as it turned out.

More Scientific Experiments

For some inexplicable reason, probably boredom, I started seeing how long I could sleep each day. I got into a pattern of getting up every morning at 7:30 a.m. and grabbing some breakfast before starting my day shift at 8 a.m. At the end of the shift at 4 p.m., I'd crawl into bed for an hour or two before waking up and having supper. Right after supper, instead of watching a movie or reading a book, I'd go back to bed and sleep until 7:30 the next morning. It was a pattern I was to repeat day after day for a few months.

I nailed a blanket over my window to keep out the 24-hour light. It got to the point where not only was I sleeping up to 15 hours a day, but I needed to sleep that long or I'd be dead on my feet. I'd allowed myself to fall into a bad living (sleeping) pattern.

I finally wised up and realized that this was stupid, so I replaced one stupid thing with another. I started doing anything I could to avoid going outdoors.

As each Main site had Department of Transport weathers observers on staff, the Radicians didn't have to go outside to get the temperatures every hour. Also, because the work area was connected to the accommodation modules by an overhead passageway, you didn't have to ever go outside unless you wanted to...and I didn't want to for some obtuse reason.

I think I ended up staying indoors for four months before I put the end to that stupid scientific experiment, as well.

The Cuban Missile Crisis

It was while I was at FOX Main that the Cuban Missile Crisis happened. The most noticeable change in our work procedures was that we doubled up on the console watch for each shift.

There are two FPS-19 radars at each station: an upper beam and a lower beam. The antennas are mounted back-to-back in the 25-foot-diameter radome and they do a 360-degree rotation every minute. Meanwhile the results are "painted" on the two "scopes" in the console room.

We normally only monitored the right-hand screen, which was the lower beam. During the Cuban Missile Crisis, however, the console was manned by two Radicians, one watching the lower beam and the other monitoring the upper beam. With both beams being intently watched, there was no preventative maintenance work being done, just mission critical repairs.

At that time, SAC (Strategic Air Command) traffic increased noticeably. I'm not sure how the people down south were reacting to the crisis or how they were taking it, but we took it very seriously. Frankly, we took it so seriously that some of us were wondering if there was going to be a south to go home to after it was all over. We considered the outside possibility of ending up stranded in the Arctic. It was a very tense two weeks.

We recognized that had the Russians attacked, our job would be over in the time it took the attacking aircraft to move from the top of the radar scopes to the bottom, maybe 30 minutes. At that point, our jobs were done.

Had that happened, we hypothesized that we would probably send out lateral aircraft to pick up the personnel from the Aux and I-sites and bring them to the Main station. Whether or not we attempted a flight south depended upon how many aircraft we had, if any, fuel, number of people, and whether there was a south to fly to.

It was sobering to speculate as to whether any attempt would be made to come and get us in case of war.

I was starting to learn Eskimo in my off-hours! (Not really.)

Talking to SAC (B-52 Bombers)

Strategic Air Command (SAC) aircraft were continually prowling the Arctic ready to strike against the "enemy" at a moment's notice. It was only the EAM (Emergency Action Message) that stopped them from going.

One of the popular nightmare scenarios at the time was that a SAC B-52 bomber would be inadvertently given the "go" signal and start World War III. These fears were built upon by a popular 1962 book entitled Fail-Safe, which was made into a movie by the same name in 1964 starring Henry Fonda.

In the movie, an electronic box has a failure, goes wonky, and displays a code that the aircraft commander then deciphers as the Go-code and sets a course to his target in Russia. No attempts to get him to turn back, including a radio conversation with the US President (Henry Fonda), can convince the aircraft commander that a terrible mistake has been made. You probably remember what happens next, and if not, I won't give away the rest of the movie in case you get a chance to view this classic sometime.

Anyone who is intimate with the real fail-safe system could only laugh at the scenario. The "fail-safe device" was not a device at all but a voice on the radio transmitting the go/no go (EAM) message. Our voices.

Often, we would transmit the EAM in the blind, meaning we didn't know if anyone was listening. This usually happened whenever the code changed. Other times we would transmit the EAM in response to a request from a SAC aircraft.

In order to avoid radio confusion when transmitting the EAM in the blind, the protocol was for the most easterly station in a sector to transmit the EAM first, then notify the next station to the west. That would continue until all stations in the sector has transmitted the EAM.

As I recall, a typical EAM message went something like this:

"Skyking, Skyking, this is Staghound Radio. Do not answer, do not answer. Silver Cup Charlie. Time, three four. Authentication, Oscar Papa. I say again. Skyking, Skyking, do not answer, do not answer. Silver Cup Charlie. Time, three four. Authentication, Oscar Papa. Staghound Out."

At the time, the EAM message consisted of a three-letter code (Silver Cup Charlie, in this case) which was the go/no go code, the time was in minutes after the hour (three four), and a two-letter authenticator (Oscar Papa). The authenticator code was tied to the minutes and was different for every minute.

Occasionally, one of the SAC aircraft would call you on the radio and ask if you had any "traffic" for them, in which case you'd transmit the EAM in the same format noted above with the exception that you'd sign off with your tactical call sign.

If you screwed up and gave the wrong authenticator code, the aircraft would be instantly on your butt with a request to *"Authenticate 05"* (or some other number). In this case, you didn't tell the aircraft to *"Stand-by one,"* you stayed silent and immediately used the day's classified code sheet which was located at the console, to authenticate the time, 05, and then broadcast the resulting two-character authenticator.

Tactical Call Signs

Each DEWLine site had its normal call sign which was usually its geographical location. For example, FOX Main's air/ground call sign when talking to commercial flights was "Hall Beach Radio" or simply "Hall Beach." Its tactical call sign when talking to SAC aircraft was "Staghound Radio." For the most part, all the stations as well as the SAC aircraft had very masculine sounding names. It was very much a macho thing.

I've had situations where a SAC aircraft would call Hall Beach Radio on 122.2 Mhz, which is the commercial aviation frequency, and ask if I could raise Staghound Radio for them. I'd ask them to "Stand-by one," then I'd flick up the switch for 122.2 Mhz radio channel and flick down the switch for the military frequency, 236.6 Mhz, lower my voice an octave (for effect) and say, *"Hunter 25, this is Staghound Radio. Go ahead."* At this point, not realizing that they were talking with the same station, they would usually ask if I had any "traffic" for them, in which case I'd pass along the Emergency Action Message.

For the most part, SAC pilots were a businesslike bunch, but I remember one time at CAM-4 when I came across a chatty pilot. Perhaps he was as bored as I was. In any event we got to chatting and I suggested that he drop in for a visit. He asked me how long our airstrip was. When I told him it was 3,500 feet, he replied that he'd have time to put the brakes on once before he ran off the end of the runway.

Needless to say, he declined my offer.

Dealing with Death

In general, the DEWLine was a fairly safe place to work and there were relatively few accidents or deaths. When deaths did occur, they were handled in a sort of macabre manner in order to help us deal with them. The following is a case in point.

Jim G was a baker at the lower camp at FOX Main. Jim worked alone on the overnight shift baking a pile of baked goods for the day shift to consume. Rumour had it that Jim's marriage was falling or had fallen apart, partly due, no doubt, to him being so far from the family.

In any event, Jim went to work one evening, completed all his chores and laid out all his baked goods, then hung himself in the kitchen using a bed sheet. He was found, hanging in the lower camp kitchen, by whoever was first in for breakfast.

Word spread like the proverbial wildfire. All Jim's handiwork from the previously evening was destroyed in case it had been tainted. Jim was wrapped up and stored in one of the antenna huts or storage buildings until he could be transported south on the next flight in a few days time.

As the reality of the situation began to sink in, so did the macabre mechanisms for dealing it. Notices appeared on the bulletin boards stating that, henceforth, we would all be issued with paper bed sheets and there was more than one announcement on the PA system informing us that there would be "no hanging around the lower camp kitchen."

Sick? I suppose. We did what we had to do to manage our own mental state.

A Movie to Remember

As I mentioned, as a general rule, we got first-run movies on the Line. One such movie was the first of the James Bond series, Dr. No.

When I first heard the title, I had no idea what the movie was about and I had no interest in seeing a medical movie so I passed on the initial showing. Bad move, as I was only able to watch it seven times instead of eight before it disappeared on its journey across the sector.

For those of you who remember the movie, there was a defining moment when James Bond (Sean Connery) sees Honey Ryder (Ursula Andress) for the first time. She comes strolling out of the water and up the beach wearing, what was for the time, a very revealing bikini. This is just the thing a bunch of guys who have been away from women for several months need to see! We went crazy!

From the second showing (which I saw) on, the movie area was packed.

Never had a movie been shown so often in so short a time and never had any movie been so well received. It was with great reluctance that we released the movie for its trip across the sector.

Chapter 6: All Good Things Must Come to an End

It was fast becoming time to move along for the last time. I could have done a couple of additional tours, but I had no real reason to do so. I'd accumulated enough money to accomplish what I wanted to do, which was go to university, and during one of my trips south, I'd met the woman, Marilyn Jacobs, who was to become my first wife and the mother of my two boys.

While there was a sense of sadness at leaving the Line, there was also a sense of adventure for what lay ahead. The DEWLine had been a major part of my life to that point. I climbed on the southbound flight for the last time without any regrets and many, many memories, all good.

I remain a DEWLiner to this day as I believe, as DEWLiner Clive Beckmann believes, that there is no such thing as a former DEWLiner. Once a DEWLiner, always a DEWLiner.

Chapter 7: Post DEWLine

Upon leaving the Line, I got married, bought a house, and went to university. University didn't work out as I realized that I was going to end up being a 50 percent engineer, so I went back to being a 90 percent electronics technician (modesty wouldn't allow me to say 100 percent).

I went back doing repair and overhaul work (once again) on military equipment (Racal RA-17's) for a company called Instronics Limited, until I moved into sales. (It was either move into sales or be fired, but that's another story!) It was a good move, and over the years I was successful enough to move into sales management and ultimately into my own company doing sales training and sales management consulting for over 45 years.

I still dabble in ham radio (VE3UU) and have a small collection of boat anchor radios from the vacuum tube era, including a Racal RA-17 receiver that I used to overhaul as a young technician.

Like many people, my first marriage didn't last. I've always considered that, for most guys, the first marriage is a training marriage. It was good while it did last, and I have two fine sons, Michael and Patrick, as a result.

I ultimately found my intended life mate, Lorraine, and with her, my wonderful step-daughter, Anita. This is a marriage that has lasted and will continue to last. We go into our golden years with six grandchildren—Allycia, Heather and Matthew from Anita's family; Aiden and Callum from Michael's family; and Cole from Patrick's family. I'm an incredibly fortunate person.

Chapter 8: The End of the Story

There is no end, at least not yet anyway. There's always another adventure out there for the taking. It's not true that "all good things must come to an end." They just keep on going for as long as you let them.

So, let the good times roll.

Postscript

Is it really the end of the story? Read on!

On June 25, 2012, I received permission from the Nasittuq Corporation and the Government of Canada to visit Hall Beach one more time. The Nasittuq Corporation is the organization that, like the old Federal Electric Corporation (FEC), managed the North Warning System (NWS) that has replaced the DEWLine.

So almost 52 years to the day after I first arrived at Hall Beach, and 49 years after I left there for what was to be the last time, my life has gone full circle. Talk about having closure!

I'm delighted now to have an opportunity to add the final chapters to this adventure.

Chapter 9:
Return to the DEWLine - 2012

The Dream

It started innocently enough, a simple dream to return to FOX Main (Hall Beach NU), the place where I had my 20th birthday, 50 years after the fact. I would be 70 in 2010.

It was 2009 when the dream started. That gave me less than a year to make it happen. The DEWLine had morphed into the North Warning System (NWS) and I had no contacts, at any level, within the Nasittuq Corporation who manages the NWS or the Government, to make this thing happen. By 2012, the dream had all but died, or so I thought.

The dream came about because for the past few years I had been in regular correspondence with fellow DEWLiners Paul Kelley in Wales UK and Lyall Lalonde in Winnipeg. Lyall and I first met at CAM-D in 1960 when he was the sector mechanic and I was the station Radician. Our paths crossed from time to time while we were on the Line.

On the other hand, Paul and I were both Radicians at FOX Main around the same time but neither of us remembers the other and we didn't connect until 2005 or so. Since then, we've been in fairly constant communication while he was documenting his time on the Line. He has an incredibly detailed tale to tell.

It was because of these contacts that I began to get the urge to "go home" again. In fact, my first home-away-from-home was CAM-4 Pelly Bay. Until I arrived at CAM-4 in August of 1960, I had lived at home with my mother. With my arrival at CAM-4 in 1960, I was now on my own and out of the nest for the first time.

Rekindled Dream

Over the years, various people would stumble over my DEWLine.ca or my VE3UU.com websites and contact me with questions and/or their stories of the DEWLine and life in the Arctic.

One such person was Mark Pimlott. At the time, Mark lived and worked in Igloolik NU, and had for many years. I'm not exactly sure how we first connected, but Mark has been kind enough to send me stuff from time to time. It was one of these pieces of 'stuff' that rekindled the dream and was instrumental in making it happen.

On May 31, 2012, Mark sent me an email with an attachment of some interpretative panels that were proposed for installation at Hall Beach. The panel included several quotes from Paul Kelley, so I forwarded it on to Paul for his reading pleasure.

Then, one day later, I received a second email from Mark containing yet another PDF, this one not only containing quotes by me but several pictures from my web site including photos of yours truly as a young Radician. In his email Mark asked if the Nunavut Parks department had asked for my permission to use my stuff on their interpretive panels. They hadn't.

The fact that they hadn't sought my permission didn't bother me as I was delighted that someone found it interesting enough to use. However, the fact that they had used my material without asking permission opened the door for me to seek their assistance in realizing my dream of visiting Hall Beach.

I sent off an email to the minister in charge of the Nunavut Parks department in an attempt to make him feel guilty enough to bring me up North. While it didn't work, the gentleman who replied, Cameron Delong, copied Jessica Hallam of the Nassituq Corporation who offered to see what could be done about arranging for a visit to FOX Main, Hall Beach NU facility. The Nassituq Corporation was the organization that managed the Northern Warning System at the time.

The Stars Align

Jessica contacted me on June 13 and let me know that she was the person who arranged things like this and that, "I have never dealt with a request of this nature, but I'll do my best."

Complicating my situation was the fact that I had been diagnosed with an aggressive form of kidney cancer in my right kidney and was slated to go into the hospital on July 17 to have the damn thing removed. This severely limited my window of opportunity in that if this visit didn't happen soon, it wasn't going to happen at all for me.

On June 18, Jessica had received approval from both the Nassituq Corporation and the Canadian government for me to visit Hall Beach. The only dates available were July 2-4. As an added bonus, the Nassituq Corporation would provide accommodations, rations, and local transportation while I was at Hall Beach.

All I had to do was arrange my own transportation north which I did within minutes of receiving Jessica's email. I would leave Ottawa via FirstAir on July 1st, overnight in Iqaluit NU, and carry on to Hall Beach on July 2nd.

Like a Child on Christmas Eve

To say that I was excited about the trip is an understatement. I couldn't have been more excited. I was like a young child on Christmas Eve, full of anticipation and expectations. Was Santa going to be good to me? Will I be allowed into the Electronic Modules where I spent most of my DEWLine work life? What do the buildings look like now? How might they have changed? What has 52 years done to the appearance of the facilities? Is the Emergency Radio Room where I operated as VE8SK still there? Might I get to operate the station one last time?

The Journey of a Lifetime (for Me)

For whatever reason, I knew that this trip was going to be a big thing in my life and I was sharp enough to keep a log or diary of the journey. What follows is an edited version of that diary with some additional observations.

Chapter 10: Trip Diary

Day 1: July 1, 2012 - Canada Day,
The Journey Begins

My wife Lorraine dropped me off at the airport in lots of time. I was so pumped that I would have slept at the airport overnight if there had been any chance of missing this flight.

As I mentioned, I was like a little kid at Christmas except, instead of waiting for Santa Claus to come down from the north, I was going north to beat him to the punch.

First Stop: Iqaluit

The trip north on FirstAir was a hell of a lot shorter and more comfortable than the one I took 52 years ago. About three hours to Iqaluit (aka Frobisher Bay in 1963) by 737-200 rather than six to seven hours in Nordair's DC-4, CF-IQM.

The flight was surprisingly full, about two-thirds, as there were a large number of students on an Arctic adventure of some sort. The FirstAir cabin service was a throwback to earlier days when cabin crews were pleasant and service oriented. The FirstAir cabin crew couldn't do enough for the passengers and their warm chocolate chip cookies are to die for.

We arrived around noon and after a three-minute, $6 cab drive, I arrived at the Capital Suites Inn. I got here in time to catch the tail end of the Canada Day parade and decided to take a walking tour around town, including a trek to the highest point of town where I took pictures of the entire town.

Iqaluit is not a big place and by 1:30 I had exhausted both my legs and the sights. I tried to have a mid-afternoon nap but my mind wouldn't shut off so I went off on another walking adventure this time bypassing the Tim Horton's coffee shop and on to the local museum and the visitor center, both of which were open and quite interesting. Timmies was closed so I couldn't compare prices although a whole watermelon in the local supermarket was advertised as being "on sale" for $14 and pineapples were $7 ea. I can only imagine what a coffee and muffin must have cost at Tim Horton's.

I'm discovering an interesting phenomenon, it seems that the DEWLine has all but disappeared from view (or interest) in this area. The few people with whom I've had a chance to share my quest were polite but basically uninterested. I supposed I shouldn't be too surprised as these days people seem to be quite self-absorbed anyways. I suspect it will be different in Hall Beach as the community lives in the shadows of a DEWLine main station, FOX Main.

I had Arctic char for supper at a nearby restaurant and, as was promised by the desk clerk at my hotel, the food was good and the service was poor. My other choices were a hotel where the service was good and the food lousy, yet another where both the food and service were good, but the prices were very high, and finally, a place where the food, service, and prices were good but the walk to get to it was long.

Tomorrow I need to get to the airport by 6:30 to catch my 7:30 flight to Igloolik and Hall Beach. I hope to get off the plane at Igloolik to shake Mark Pimlott's hand as he's the guy who started this by sending me the information on the proposed Hall Beach interpretive panel that had my pictures on it.

Day 2: July 2, 2012 - On to Hall Beach

The plane should have left 20 minutes ago but the fog is very bad and I have no idea when we will leave nor is anyone saying anything as yet. The departures board still shows the flight as being 'on-time.'

Seeing as I was awake early, I decided to walk over to the airport from the hotel rather than make a further investment in the Iqaluit economy by taking a $6 cab ride. The walk over took about 10 minutes in the quiet morning fog. I was the first passenger at the terminal this morning. There are probably about 30 of us here now waiting for the fog to lift. I overheard one person saying that they are on their fourth day here waiting for good weather at their destination. I know the weather at my destination is good; it's the weather at my departure point, Iqaluit, that's the problem.

This isn't looking good.

Arriving at Hall Beach

We finally took off at 9:00 am but were unable to land in Igloolik due to poor weather at that site. The entire flight of two hours was eventless as we were above the clouds. My seatmate was a six-seven-year-old aboriginal boy who, like every child of that age, was a bundle of pent-up perpetual motion. I think I have bruises on my right leg from his continual kicking of it. He was lucky to get off the plane unharmed!

The plane was a French/Italian ATR-42 and was half cargo and half passenger (20 of us including the obligatory nursing aboriginal!). Cabin service included a plastic version of the paper box lunch I had for my first trip 52 years ago.

Here's another quirk of fate. The aircraft registration for my first trip north was CF-IQM. The registration of today's aircraft was C-FIQU. One letter different. Go figure.

I didn't realize that we had missed landing at Igloolik until we began landing and I saw the radome and troposcatter antennas. I thought it was a bit strange until I realized that we were landing at Hall Beach, and not Igloolik.

The old hanger is still there but decommissioned and is now used for storage. Unlike in 1960, there is now an actual terminal building in place of the USAF blue school bus that we used to deplane into. I was met at the 'airport' by the station maintenance person, Gerald Walsh, who brought me up to the main building where I met Rick Chaulk, the site manager, otherwise known as "God." Rick is a charming Newfoundlander who instantly made me feel welcome and who will be giving me a tour after lunch.

First Look Around (in 52 years!)

I had an incredible afternoon. Rick Chaulk, the site manager couldn't have been more accommodating and pleasant. It's almost like having a visitor is a welcomed diversion from their daily grind.

Unfortunately, all three of the sector electronic maintenance technicians are off site doing preventative maintenance at the various sites under FOX Main's control. Their responsibility runs from CAM-4, Pelly Bay, on the west, now CAM-4A as the original site has been razed, to FOX-CA which replaced FOX-C, to the east. There are now Long Range Radars (LRR's) at CAM-3, FOX Main, and FOX-3 with Short Range Radars (SRR's) in between at CAM-D, CAM-4A, CAM-5A, CAM-FA, FOX-1, FOX-A, FOX-2, FOX-B, and FOX-CA.

Interesting side note, whereas in our day we had six to eight technical people (Radicians) per site, or about 50 technicians for the entire sector (seven sites), now the sector only has three technicians. They fly them out by helicopter whenever something goes wrong. Almost all the sites are totally unmanned and remotely monitored in North Bay and at FOX Main. No more daily lateral flights, just helicopter flights on an as-needed basis.

Marion Rocko, the site's facilities manager, took me on a driving tour around the site and into the community of Hall Beach which is about six kilometres north of the main site. It's a bit sad to see the conditions of the community. There is little to no sign of community pride. Things are left everywhere. Buildings are in disrepair or derelict. What new buildings there were looked like they were on their way to a similar state of disrepair.

Marion was kind enough to take a number of photos with me in them so at least I'll have some proof of actually being here.

Marion is the gentleman in charge of the power generation plant and took me on a tour of their power plant. If I remember correctly, they have six generators, three of which are about 230Kw and 3 around 177Kw. The remote sites all have three Lister diesel generators. Only one generator is required to power the site. Should one generator fail, the second one immediately comes alive and an alarm is sent. The third generator is there in case the second one has a problem. Triple redundancy. As the remote sites are unmanned, they don't need to have the lights on until someone shows up to do work so the power requirements are modest.

Marion also drove up to the top of the berm where all the toxic waste had to be disposed of at a horrendous cost. There is a plaque on it. Apparently, there is a fabulous plaque at the location where CAM-4 used to be. The site has been wiped off the face of the earth and the site now stands as a model of cleaning up a technological mess and returning the land to pristine condition.

The news of the demise of CAM-4 saddened me because, as I've mentioned, CAM-4 (Pelly Bay) was my first real home-away-from-home. Now it is no more. It felt like I had lost a bit of personal history.

Accommodations

During the latter part of the afternoon I had free run of the buildings, so I went around taking photos of everything. I'm in a VIP accommodation. What they have done is taken several of the room pairs and knocked out the adjoining wall to double the size of the room. So, basically, my current room is twice the size of my former room in 1963. The arrangement gives you a double bed instead of a single, and a sitting room with a very comfortable easy chair. Many of the rooms have TV service as well.

Fortunately, I'm on a northerly facing bedroom so the 24 hours daylight won't be too bad. If I'm up, I may go out around midnight just to take a photo.

The Electronic Modules

The last thing that I did this afternoon was to have a tour of the "Operations Area" in the former Electronics modules. As you recall, this was one of my hidden hopes. Rick asked if I still held a 'secret' clearance and I assured him that I did as I've done nothing to lose it and it doesn't have to be renewed.

As one might expect, all the rooms have been repurposed and none of the original equipment, or even signs of the original equipment, are there. The Console Room where every Radician, and in later days, Console Operators, would have spent at least four hours a day, is now one large room instead of two and all remnants of the communication centre gear and console equipment have long disappeared.

As the Operations Area is still considered confidential, I won't be outlining what I saw in each of the rooms. If you're a former DEWLiner and you're curious, contact me by email.

As you might imagine, it was quite a thrill for me to revisit the area where I spent so much of my time as a Radician during 1960-63. Probably only another DEWLiner would understand how I felt.

I asked about the Emergency Radio Room which originally contained amateur radio equipment and, as expected, it is long gone as is the need for such equipment. Satellite and telephones have replaced the need for HF radio equipment.

End of a Long day

The canteen, such as it is, was open just prior to supper so I purchased the obligatory souvenirs to take home with me.

Supper was good but not great. There was lots of it though and more desserts than you can shake a stick at. It wouldn't take long to put on extra weight if you weren't careful. You can go to the dining area at any time, day or night, for a bowl full of ice cream, piece of pie or cake, and the coffee's always on. The coffee isn't always as fresh as one might want but it's always there.

After supper I met one of the site's three meteorological (weather) people in the recreation area. He was a chatty fellow and pretty well filled me in on what's what in the Met department.

The old meteorological buildings are still there but only used for storage at this point as the Met people now work out of the airport terminal building. The Met people are no longer government employees but work for a private, for-profit company that provides the service under contract. Each of the three people provide all three services: upper air atmospheric measurements, weather observations, and handle air/ground radio communications for the airport.

Of the three Met people, only two are on the site at any given time. The two that are here work one long day (15 hours) on and one day off on a rotational basis. They spend eight weeks up here and then go south for four weeks. The eight weeks here and then four weeks down south schedule seem to be the standard rotation for many people on the site. This is far different from earlier times when you spent six months, or more, here and two weeks off.

One other interesting phenomenon - the site is basically empty. Apart from the five RCMP officers who arrived to investigate a local stabbing, there were probably no more than 10-15 people around. I had the recreation module pretty well to myself for most of the evening. It seemed a bit surreal to be lounging in an easy chair, watching television, 1800 miles north of home.

Day 3: July 3, 2012 - First Full Day

Despite closing what curtains I have on the windows of my north westerly facing bedroom, the midnight sun still lit up my room making it difficult to sleep. Part of the difficulty is my continued excitement at just being here.

I stayed up until just after 11pm as I wanted to get a shot of the midnight sun. Even a photo doesn't do the phenomenon justice; you must experience it in person for the full effect.

Upon awakening from what little sleep I did get, I discovered two problems. One, the fog outside made it difficult to see from one end of the module train to the other and, two, I neglected to bring a towel with me and none are provided at Hotel FOX Main. No shower for me! Drying oneself with paper towels presents an interesting challenge.

The fog is going to put a crimp on my sightseeing adventures unless it burns off. Even more importantly, it could put a big crimp in tomorrow's travel plans as I'm due to return south.

After an excellent breakfast, I attended the 8 AM station briefing where the day's activities were outlined. With the exception of one sick person, everyone was there including the site maintenance person and cook, for a total of eight people. Eight people on a site that in earlier times held 50 or more. Eerie. I suspect that there may be another half dozen workers around, probably seasonal folks, as the occasional strange face pops up from time to time.

Weather permitting, we're expecting a FirstAir Hercules aircraft in later today for an airlift of material to FOX-3. That's expected to take several days. Much of the cargo will be POL (fuel for the generators).

I'm not sure what today will bring. With the fog being as thick as it is, it will be unsafe to wander around the site as once you are out of sight of landmarks, you would have no idea as to where you are and which direction you should go. Let's hope it burns off before mid-day.

I was chatting with Marion this morning before the station briefing and he was explaining the political situation to me. Nasittuq's contract has expired and they are operating on an extension while the project goes out to tender. Both Raytheon and SNC-Lavalin want to bid on the contract so Nasittuq has been cutting costs where they can in order to hold on to the contract. As one might expect, this process has had an impact on people's morale.

Unlike the early years, the place is unionized. People have to keep time sheets and are paid overtime when appropriate. The battle to keep costs low has meant that preventative maintenance is kept to a minimum and the emphasis is on corrective maintenance.

On a more pleasant note, people have been very accommodating and while I'm obviously an outsider, I've been made to feel very welcome.

I suspect that by tomorrow morning I will have seen everything I wanted to see and more and I'll be ready to come home with a brain full of memories.

Exploring the Module Trains

As the site is still enclosed in the fog, I decided to explore the part of the B-train that contained the former power generators. As I remember the area, there was a movie area just before the power generator modules. As you leave the inter-module train overpass and turn to the right, that immediate area is now the site admin offices. These were previously located in A-train modules. As you go down the corridor past the offices and where the old movie area was, you go into where the generators were located. You can see the change of flooring from wood to concrete. These modules now contain an extensive set of exercise equipment, weights, treadmills, punching bag, and various forms of personal torture devices known as exercise machines.

As you go even further deeper into this area there is an entrance way to the newly added waste-water recycling module that is located aside the end of the module train. I was given a tour of the equipment by Rick.

I must point out that I had never been in this part of the module train in earlier times. Only the station mechanics would have been allowed in there.

Going even further into this area you come across an enclosed ventilated "smoker's lounge" that contains a bunch of easy chairs, large television, fake fireplace from the old military officer's lounge of years ago, a big bar fridge, and sundry supplies for your recreational pleasure.

Finally, the last modules contain some equipment that I didn't recognize but seemed to have to do with water. Oh yes, there is also a sauna in this area as well. All the comforts of home… well sort of.

As for being the 'only' visitor, I'm not sure I'm the only one but I know that it is a rarity. Rick was contacted before I received my permission and asked if it was okay for me to come. Fortunately for me, he said yes. It seems that the site manager has the last word, or at least a say in who 'visits.'

By 11 AM the fog is still showing no sign of lifting any time soon which makes the time go on forever. I took my video camera and did a stroll down most of the interiors of the A- and B-train as well as the dining area. (Footnote: I was able to combine the video footage and some still shots into a video of the trip titled, "Hall Beach: Fifty Years Later, An Old Dewliner's Pilgrimage." You can watch the video slideshow at http://Vimeo.com/59763364. It's also on YouTube as well. As of 2018, the YouTube video has had over 16,000 views. It hasn't exactly gone viral but at least someone's seen it.)

The weather may also play havoc with the arrival of the FirstAir Hercules. We'll see. Having explored most of the inside of the building, I'm passing some time watching TV (would you believe?). I still hope to visit the Met office if possible.

Exploring Outside

The fog lifted enough for me to go exploring and it's now official. I've now done more walking around this site in the last day and a half than I did during the three years I was in and out of this place in the early 60s! I never walked to or from the airport back then. I did it twice today and may do it one more time if the Hercules that is due in here in about an hour actually arrives.

The fog has been in and out all day. At one point it appeared to have generally cleared up so I walked out to the two large tropospheric antennas with the plan of climbing to the top to take a picture of the site. By the time I got there, the fog had rolled in again and you couldn't see the site from the antennas at all.

At 90 feet tall, I decided that climbing the antennas would be folly at my age, so I took a pass on that part of the adventure activities.

While on my first trip to the airfield, I stopped off at the old/new Met building. (Old because it isn't used anymore and 'new' because it wasn't there in 1963.) Imagine my surprise when I found the door open and an even greater surprise when I found someone in it. It was the off-duty Met guy who was using the building as a smoke room and a place to do some paper work. He showed me around the abandoned building as well as the hydrogen building where they still launch the weather balloons twice a day at 7:15 AM and 7:15 PM along with another 1100 sites worldwide.

I trooped back to the airport and visited the resident Met manager and gave him a thumb drive containing pictures from the old Met station in 1963. I tried to use the thumb drive to bribe him to arrange for good weather for tomorrow. I'm not sure it worked. We'll see tomorrow.

Everything in the Met office is automated except the visual observations. No more Stevenson screens with their wet and dry bulb thermometers. Progress.

I believe I just heard the Hercules aircraft land or maybe do a missed approach. Lots of noise. It appears that the weather at the approach end of the runway was good enough for the aircraft to land.

Day 4: July 4, 2012 - Time to Leave (Again)

The weather at Hall Beach is bright and sunny, but then it's always sunny at this time of the year. You just can't always see it. If the weather in Iqaluit is good, then the chances of my leaving today are very good.

For me, it has been an incredible and powerful journey. So powerful in fact that my eyes are watering at the thought of leaving the Arctic for the very last time. Hell, I never thought I'd have a second opportunity to leave here for the 'last' time.

The pace of the last two days has been such that I've truly been able to recapture the feelings I had during the first stay 50 some odd years ago. I've fit right into the pace and pulse of the station and I've found myself bored from time to time. Certainly, the recreational activities are much better, and it was a bit surreal to sit in the recreation module and watch TV much like I might do at home. It's even odder when I realize that some of the people have their own TVs in their rooms.

There is no doubt that the more humane work schedule of eight weeks on site and four weeks down south, coupled with the double-sized room makes life up here much more endurable.

I have been able to identify one of the major benefits of this trip for me and that is that it has removed the lingering question that I've had about this place, without really realizing I had it. Hadn't I made this trip, I would have always wondered about this place and what was becoming of it. Now I know.

The plan for the area is to maintain the buildings and facilities until 2020. Although the buildings are in surprisingly good condition, unless they do something beyond normal maintenance, that is all they can reasonably expect.

The plan for today is to get my picture taken with the two to three people who have been most helpful and gracious to me during my visit. I also want to get a photo of the Met office at the airport for Paul Kelley. I owe Nassituq an article for their company newsletter so that will be on my mind. As I've crawled and walked over every inch of the place over the past few days there isn't much more for me to explore.

With the possible exception of a former DEWLiner, few people would ever understand why such a journey would be so meaningful to me.

Final Observations

As one might expect, these are different times, 52 years of difference. Attitudes are different. There is a sense of cheerlessness here now. It's not that everyone was walking around grumbling, it was more a lack of laughter, a lack of cheer. People were doing their jobs and doing them willingly and with dedication, but they are just that, jobs. In our day, and more importantly, our times, there was a sense that we were part of something bigger, important, and critical. Hell, we were part of the Cold War!

I also believe that the eight-in four-out schedule doesn't foster the same kinship that a bunch of people develop when stuck in an isolated location for six to eight months at a time does, particularly when you are truly out of touch with 'home.' Now, access to television, the Internet, daily commercial flights, and better communications have totally removed the sense of isolation.

Inuit Wisdom

While I was waiting at the airport for the flight home, one of the site Inuit asked if I was the "Old DEWLiner" who was visiting. (Apparently the word got around.) After assuring him that I didn't know his father or cousin who used to work on the site in earlier years, we got to speculating about how long the site, and the jobs, might be around.

He suggested that maybe someone should start another Cold War. Interesting thought!

Southward Bound

It been forty-nine years since I last left Hall Beach and now I'm leaving it for the last time. It has been an incredible trek down memory lane for me and one that I will never forget.

I hope you enjoyed taking the nostalgic journey with me.

The Final Chapter: Historical Timeline

Here, as near as I can recollect and reconstruct, is the timeline of my adventures in the Arctic.

Month 1: Apr 1960. Hired by FEC and sent to Streator, Ill for training.

Month 4: Jul 60. Arrived at Hall Beach (FOX Main) NWT.

Month 5: Aug 60. Celebrate my 20th birthday and then shipped off to CAM-4.

Month 8: Dec 60. Christmas at the Pelly Bay Mission.

Month 14: May 61. Nine-month anniversary. R & R* time. Postponed R & R until August.

Month 17: Aug 61. Two weeks R & R leave. Assigned to CAM-D upon my return.

Month 20: Nov 61. Formal EOC*. Postponed until mid-January.

Month 22: Jan 62. Six weeks EOC leave.

Month 24: Mar 62. Start of second contract. Assigned to the FOX sector crew.

Month 27: Jun 62. Replaced Phil Collins at FOX-3.

Month 28: Jul 62. Acting Station Chief at FOX-C.

Month 29: Aug 62: Polar bear hunt at FOX -1.

Month 30: Sep 62. Two weeks R & R leave. Assigned to FOX Main upon my return.

Month 31: Oct 62. Cuban Missile Crisis.

Month 36: Mar 63. Left the DEWLine for the last time on my final EOCL*.

52 Years later, July 2012. Returned to FOX Main, Hall Beach, for a trip down memory lane.

* Definitions:
R & R = Rest & Recreation (mid-contract vacation)
EOC = End of Contract
EOCL = End of Contract leave

Major assignments:
- At CAM-4 from August 1960 to August 1961;
- At CAM-D from August 1961 to January 1962;
- On the FOX Sector Crew from March 1962 to September 1962;
- Acting Station Chief, FOX-C from June 1962 to July 1962.
- Lateral Radician at FOX Main from September 1962 until leaving the Line in March 1963.

About the Author

After Brian left the DEWLine in 1963, he continued to work as an electronics technician for several years before transitioning into technical sales, ultimately getting into sales training and starting his own sales training business with his wife Lorraine.

Brian and Lorraine became inadvertent serial entrepreneurs, having started and sold four companies. Their current company, number five, is Quintarra Consulting Inc, and specializes in sales management consulting.

At 78, Brian is slowing down and spends more time doing social volunteering than consulting. He is a volunteer Crisis Team Leader at the Ottawa Distress Center and volunteer Guide (Docent) at the Diefenbunker, Canada's Cold War Museum, amongst other endeavors.

Brian and Lorraine continue to live outside the small village of Carp Ontario, a suburb of Ottawa, Canada's capital.

Brian can be reached by email at:

BrianJeffrey@Xplornet.com
or Brian@VE3UU.com.

Be sure to visit his personal DEWLine website at www.DEWLINE.ca as well as Larry Wilson's omnibus DEWLine website at http://lswilson.dewlineadventures.com.

Brian's amateur radio website is at www.VE3UU.com.

August 2018.

CAM-D 1961. Brian holding the baby he almost had to deliver.

Carp 2018. Brian still enjoys playing around with ham radio.